The Weight of Birds

ISBN Paperback 978-1-7348052-3-9
ISBN Kindle E-Book 978-1-7348052-9-1

To Kristen,

my faithful cheerleader who read every version

of this story with gusto and enthusiasm.

Also by Amanda Lewis:

George – A Short,

Unconventional Story

About A Short,

Unconventional Man

For he shall give his angels charge over thee,

to keep thee in all thy ways.

Psalm 91:11

The Weight of Birds

By Amanda Lewis

Prologue

The hazy, soft lighting cast a *sfumato* glow on all surfaces in the restaurant. My art history professor would be proud of me for remembering what that word meant. I caught the scent of leather once again as Peter hung his jacket on the back of his chair. Charlie had somehow always managed to smell like apple pie. A strand of Peter's slicked back, golden hair dislodged itself. He casually reached up to swipe it back into place. He had seemed so proper just hours before.

"It's unusual for a photographer with expertise such as yours to arrive unannounced," Peter began. "Typically, there are whispers in the industry for months before an artist moves here. What brought you to New York?"

I tugged at my blouse, my face flushing slightly. I didn't like to talk about Charlie with people I barely knew.

"I'm a widow."

Chapter 1

I had never seen anyone glow. My daddy always said the first time he saw my mama, she was glowing. Daddy had fallen off the back ramp of his truck while unloading it at work and banged his head pretty good. Mama had been the nurse that tended to him. He said she radiated light, and he knew right then she was the one. Mama said he was just concussed.

When my parents got married, they decided to start their life in a little town called Vidalia. Then they had me a few short years later. And then a few short years after that, I met my husband Charlie. After high school, we moved to Savannah to officially start our life and open my gallery. For ten years he was in my life. He was mine, and I was his. And then he was gone. I didn't know I'd be a widow by age twenty-five.

I could hear the hysteria in Brad's voice in the background while Shelly talked. Charlie had gone out to play basketball with Brad and some of the other husbands from our Sunday school class. I had to go check on something at the gallery, so we had agreed to meet up for dinner later.

Charlie had collapsed during the game and had been rushed to the ER. They didn't yet know what had happened, it was all so fast. Only twenty minutes ago Charlie was talking smack, winning the game. Then he was being loaded into the back of an ambulance. I was running before I hung up the phone. My stomach was in knots.

Something was wrong. *Everything* felt wrong. I didn't know what to think as I ran the short distance to the hospital. The wind was blowing too hard. I stumbled as it shoved me. The air was wrong. It felt heavy and disgusting and vile. I caught the smell of rotten fish from the river. I couldn't see straight as I walked into the ER waiting room. Through tears, I saw Brad and Shelly holding each other and crying. It was a brain aneurysm. He had felt no pain as he collapsed into death, and then he was gone. Charlie was pronounced dead at 3:02. He was only twenty-seven.

I rushed to his side, and cradled his head in my arms. He looked like he was sleeping, his beautiful face at peace. I kissed his cold lips as my tears fell onto his eyelashes.

"Charlie, please don't do this. Please don't leave me," I sobbed.

Charlie was young, active and healthy. That's the thing about aneurysms; they don't care who they take. They just take, selfishly. Charlie and I decided long ago that we would both be organ donors. We were adamant that if something ever happened to either of us, we wanted our organs to hopefully do some good for others and make a difference in the world. I think I signed some papers agreeing to donate his organs, but I barely remember any other details from that day.

I buried him in his denim jacket, the one he was wearing when I first saw him. The first time I ever saw someone glow. It was his favorite article of clothing for some reason, and he could make it look fabulous no matter what the fashion trends were. It only felt right that he should wear it. I kept his wedding ring, and wore it on a chain around my neck.

I laid him to rest in Bonaventure Cemetery, underneath a massive oak tree with Spanish moss. After the funeral was over, I stayed and tried to say a final goodbye. I set a small replica of *The Bird Girl* beside his headstone, thinking he would appreciate it. Through my tears, I chuckled. I wanted him to be able to look down and smile at our life together. As I wiped my tears away, a heavy wind enveloped me. A seagull with no right foot and a heart shaped scratch on his beak was perched a few headstones over.

The next few months that followed were mostly a blur to me. I refused to believe Charlie was really gone. Consumed with grief and depression, I visited his graveside frequently. I took my camera with me like a security blanket. I kept thinking maybe his spirit would appear to me in photos, and I would understand that he was on the other side. He never showed.

It was hard for me to keep the gallery going alone. It was hard to do anything. Every day was a struggle. I had to go back to working at the Cotton Exchange during the weekdays. I only had my gallery open on the weekends when there was more foot traffic. Nobody really shops for photographs on a Tuesday afternoon anyway. The waitressing money was decent, but I knew why. I would frequently hear whispers from the locals. "Is that the widow girl?" "She's so young." "I wonder if she knew it was coming." "Were there any signs?" "Let's leave her an extra dollar." "She looks like she's going to cry."

My mom offered me my old room, but I couldn't go back to Vidalia. Charlie wouldn't want that for me. We had worked so hard and come so far with the little bit that we had, I felt I would betray him if I turned back and gave up. I found a therapy group for young widows and widowers, but that only irritated me and made me even more upset. I was angry all the time. I was angry at the life that I was living, angry at Charlie for leaving me alone, and angry at God for taking him from me. How could this happen? How could this happen to us? God had led us into each other's lives, and this was the ending? For what? Charlie's death was pointless and unnecessary.

I cried myself to sleep on nights when I could fall asleep. At first there were good dreams, reliving the events in our life exactly as they had been.

We'd been married in June, a month after I graduated high school. I was eighteen and he was twenty. We had a simple yet elegant wedding at a barn just outside of town, country chic. My dress was something I had found at a vintage store. It was floor-length with lace sleeves and a lace collar, satin covered buttons lined up the back. Charlie wore his nicest shirt, cream-colored, with light tan pants, which matched our vintage theme beautifully.

The pastor pronounced us husband and wife at 3:01. There had been thunderstorms off and on all week, so we played it safe and had candles and tealights inside Mason jars for decorations instead of anything too elaborate in case of a monsoon. We bought a whole slew of disposable cameras and let our guests be the ones to photograph our wedding day through their eyes. It started raining after we'd said our vows, so after everyone finished eating we danced. Despite the rain and the humidity, we all danced the night away. The mud made for some hilarious photos of ourselves and our guests. Muddy, ruined outfits adorned each and every one. No one had a care in the world. The whole day was loving and delicious and joyous and perfect. Then I would wake up.

Other times, I would dream of moments we'd spent together. We were members of the Telfair Museum, and we would regularly go and sit for hours imagining stories about the paintings and statues, what the subjects must've been thinking to hold this pose or have that expression.

Charlie's favorite statue was *The Bird Girl.* "I wonder how she feels with the weight of the birds on her shoulders?" Then he would laugh at his clever pun, which wasn't really that clever. I fell more in love with him every time he laughed. Anytime he got tickled, his face would scrunch up. First, the lines around his eyes would crinkle up and he'd start with a chuckle, which would snowball into a full belly laugh complete with his eyes tightly shut and his lower jaw bouncing up and down. Whenever we disagreed, which was rare, I always knew if he was serious or not. The crinkles around his eyes would give him away in an instant. It's funny, the details you remember. I remember thinking he was going to be the cutest little old man someday, sitting in a rocking chair on our front porch laughing and laughing at his corny jokes.

Sometimes if we had a few daylight hours, we would go and feed the seagulls down by the water. We'd buy some birdseed and a loaf of bread from the store, but it was never enough. It's a little-known fact that if seagulls are in the area, a person can throw out bread in an empty parking lot, and dozens of seagulls will almost instantly appear out of nowhere. It was cheap and fun, so it had quickly become one of our regular activities for as long as we'd been together. We even fed the seagulls instead of going to both our junior and senior prom. We didn't want to spend unnecessary money on glitz and glamour when we already knew what our future held.

The seagulls have "gull scouts," another of Charlie's hilariously punny jokes, that they send out to find food. When one of them spots the food, in a matter of minutes the area will be swarmed with a hundred seagulls or more. Small clusters of them would flap in synchronized formation just in front of us and we'd throw pieces up for them to catch mid-air. They never seemed to get full.

One seagull in particular always showed up. He had a heart-shaped scratch on his beak and no right foot. He'd sit over to the side, away from the crowd. I felt bad for him so I would give him his own piece of bread. We speculated how he might've lost his foot and Charlie decided that he was a major in the Great Gull War and lost it flying in front of his squadron, shielding them from the beaks of the onslaught. I named him Major Birdie Biddle. I woke up at the same place each time, right as Major Biddle starts pecking the piece of bread.

Soon, even pleasant dreams were tortuous. Sometimes I "sleep dream," as Charlie called it. I think I have always done it, since I was a child. I'll wake up, completely coherent, and see spiders or snakes or something in the bedroom, as real as can be. Or I wake up and think I'm somewhere else entirely. Charlie used to laugh at me because once I woke up and thought I was in a magical castle, and I tried to climb through the wall with no success.

On one night in particular, I woke up to the sound of clanging in the kitchen. I smelled bacon and coffee, and I saw a light coming from the other room. I woke up and walked in the kitchen, and there was Charlie, standing at the stove cooking bacon and chocolate gravy, a Southern delicacy, in his Star Wars pajama bottoms. He looked up and smiled at me, and I could see those precious crinkles in the corners of his eyes.

I started crying because I thought he was dead, but it had all been just a dream. I went to get some plates. I shouldn't have turned away from him. Maybe I could've kept him there longer.

As I reached up, I heard him say, "no, love."

I turned around. Only darkness was around me. The plate fell from my hands, shattering instantly on the floor. I collapsed beside it, uncontrollably shaking and sobbing for the rest of the night.

The more it set in that Charlie was really gone, the more my dreams turned into nightmares. Once I dreamed that I crashed my car off a bridge. As I plummeted down, down into the murky shallows, I could see Charlie on the bank. He was reaching for me, trying to grab my hand. The morning sun rose behind him, and I tried to reach out to him, reach for the light that was with him, but my clothes were too heavy. I was pulled down, down with the current and the fish until I couldn't see him anymore. I awoke in a cold sweat, gasping for air. Another time I dreamed that I'd never known my precious husband. I was in an alternate reality; my life had gone nothing as I had planned. I didn't recognize my surroundings or any of the people around me. I had four children, but I didn't love or even like my husband. He was mean, abusive and cold. I was repressed and depressed, stuck in a hell of spiraling sadness. I awoke from that dream sweating, screaming in anger.

I stayed in Savannah almost two years after Charlie passed. I was a shell of the woman I had been before. I couldn't seem to move on. I would see Charlie wherever I went. He was there, in the people I knew and in the faces of strangers. I felt like I'd never stop grieving. We had life insurance policies in case anything ever happened. I saved the money for quite a while, unsure of what I should do with it. It wasn't even my money, it was blood money. Life money. I would gladly trade it to have my husband back.

Shelly took me out for lunch on my twenty-seventh birthday, a number that was hard for me to comprehend since I felt betrayed by it. My fearless and feisty best friend, the thing I came to treasure about Shelly over the years is that she's a realist. She calls it as she sees it, and she's not afraid to hurt feelings if it gets the job done.

"C," she said, "I love you. You know I do, but I need to tell you something. Brad and I are worried about you. I know it's hard for you, I don't even want to imagine how hard, which is why I'm going to say what I'm about to say. You're my best friend, but honestly, you need to move. I will miss you, but I don't see the strength and creativity in you that I used to see. You would be better off if you moved away to somewhere that doesn't remind you of him." I wondered where she was going with this, her words sounded like a loaded gun.

I opened my mouth to protest. She continued, ignoring me defiantly. "It's been nearly two years. Brad and I can see you withering away. Everything that makes you the bright and beaming Cecelia Sweeting either died with Charlie or is barely hanging on to the Spanish moss for survival. Which we both know is not a pleasant thing to hang on to. You and Charlie had planned to move to New York, so do that. It'll be a fresh start."

She held my gaze as I sat in silence, taking in what she'd just said. She pounced again. "And in case you say no, I have two plane tickets to New York—one for you and one for me—for two weeks next month. Your birthday present is that we're going to be two ladies gallivanting around New York City looking for your new gallery. I also have a cousin who lives in New York, and he's willing to be our tour guide. Bonus point, if you find somewhere that works out for you, you'll already have a built-in friend close by."

Shelly placed her hands on my shoulders and looked me squarely in the eyes. "You need to quit that silly waitress job and come with me. I know that you need this, and I know Charlie would want it for you, so it won't do you any good to argue. The tickets are nonrefundable. It's time for you to start living again. We're doing this. This is happening." All I could do was stare at her while I processed what she said.

Shelly placed her hands on her hips. "Brad and I will come to visit, so you obviously don't need to stay here for us since that's what's really holding you back," she said with a smirk and a toss of her head. I could hardly argue. She was 100 percent right. I had been thinking the same thing for weeks now. Charlie wouldn't have wanted to see me this way. That's not what we worked so hard to achieve. He would've wanted me to move on with my life and our plans. I called Mama that night to talk to her about it. Apparently, Shelly had already done that too, and Mama was waiting on my phone call. "Honey, you need to go. You've lost your light. Charlie would be so mad at you for giving up and quitting your dreams. He'd kick your tail if he knew you were letting anyone, especially him, stand in your way."

She had already started packing her suitcase (six weeks early, because she likes to plan) and was prepared to come and watch my gallery for me while I was gone. All that I had to do was quit my waitressing job. I turned in my notice the next week to the owner. He hugged me and said not to take it personally, but he was glad to see me move on with my life. I wasn't close to him, but that little nudge of encouragement from someone watching from the outside was the final boost I needed to make me feel confident that I was making the right decision.

Chapter 2

Six weeks later, Shelly and I flew to New York. She asked her cousin, Roger O'Rourke, to meet us at the airport. He had lived in New York City for about twelve years. He was a fun, feisty Irishman with red hair to match Shelly's. After she introduced us, I noticed I had a hard time catching some of what he said. When he got excited, his Irish accent got heavier and heavier until all I could do was stare at him and smile.

Roger was Shelly's mother's brother's son, born and raised in Carlingford. Shelly had spent a lot of time in Ireland as a kid, so they had been close ever since childhood. Roger had been in several Broadway plays and in his spare time wrote a food blog about up and-coming restaurants in the boroughs, so he knew his way around the city.

In the taxi from the airport, Shelly squealed with delight. "Have you heard of Adelaide Andrews, the Broadway star?" she asked.

"She lives a few doors down from Roger!"

Roger rolled his eyes. He was not as impressed with this fact as Shelly was. "She watches Roger's cat, Ollie, for him when he's out of town. He says she's super nice. It's a real shame what happened."

I had heard of her, only because she and her husband had had a nasty public divorce scandal. I didn't much follow the Broadway or movie world, but I did know who her ex-husband was. His name was Travis Andrews, and he had been in a movie with my favorite actor of all time, the charismatic and charming Chris Powers.

Shelly continued to talk about random celebrity gossip until we reached the real estate agent's office, Roger humoring her along the way. I just tried to act mildly interested because I had no clue who she was talking about.

We found the perfect building in the Meatpacking District. It was a beautiful old building just begging to be turned into a gallery. The rent was affordable, and there was a studio apartment above it, meaning I wouldn't have to leave to go to work—a personal goal I had dreamt of achieving. To the right was a mirror image building with a mirror image apartment on the second floor, but it was currently not for sale.

The downstairs had an exquisite industrial feel to it, with floorto-ceiling front windows on the bottom floor for displaying, or in my case, natural lighting. An old bell hung above the door to alert of new arrivals. Old bricks and mortar lined the walls of an open floor plan, with iron pillars holding up the ceiling for stability. Copper pipes ran along and across the ceiling for the plumbing and the old heating and air system. Old wooden slats that looked like they could've been from old whiskey barrels lined the floors.

Tin panels dotted with tinges of green from oxidation lined the ceiling which added to the vintage charm. With all its merits, I couldn't believe the space was still vacant. Anyone opening a steampunk bar or nightclub would've snatched it up in a heartbeat without having to redecorate. The only thing I had to do was install some Edison style chandeliers, to ramp up the industrial appeal...and do some significant dusting.

The upstairs was just as fabulous as the first level, but completely different and spectacular in its own right. A hidden entrance was located outside, with a staircase leading up to my apartment on the left. When I walked in, I was immediately happy. I believe the energy a room gives off can change a person's mood and emotions. The lighter and more spacious the room, the more comfortable a person will feel in it. Likewise, the darker and more cramped the room, the more depressed a person will be.

The brick walls were all painted white upstairs, but the same beautiful copper pipes and wooden slat floors were visible. The same tin panels as below lined the ceiling, which were painted white like the walls to make the room appear bigger. As soon as I walked in, about four steps in front of me was the kitchen area, featuring a marble island, reasonably updated appliances, and a gas range stove.

To the left was an open area, which I planned to make into a combination living room/dining area, with plenty of room for my couch, TV, and table with four chairs. The entire left wall, also like the ground floor, was vintage glass panes, with a door opening out to a small balcony overlooking the street and the Hudson River. Beside the kitchen was an *L*-shaped hallway with two bedrooms and a bathroom in between them. These rooms were primarily behind the kitchen, so the floor pattern was like a *C* shape. The apartment was perfect, and for the first time in a very long time I felt excited.

Most importantly, this building was in budget. I had spent the weeks leading up to our flight closely analyzing my financials, my current income, commissions, and life insurance money. I had not spent one penny of the life insurance yet. My waitressing money had paid off the small amount of debt we'd had when Charlie died. I was currently debt-free and only had to worry about rent and living expenses.

I based my budget on the budget I had in Savannah, careful to factor in extra cost of living for New York rent. If I could maintain at least the volume of sales I had in Savannah, then I would be moderately successful. I was racking up bonus adulting points for not having to commute to work now. I kept thinking: this is New York, where the magic happens and anything is possible. I was willing to bet I could get my sales up at least a small percentage more with the right marketing and advertising.

After getting all the details settled with my new landlord, Shelly and I flew back to Savannah, our minds ablaze with possibilities. An accomplished stained-glass artist, she had decided to loan me some of her pieces. They would help fill my new ample floor space, as well as take full advantage to make a beautiful display in the floor-to-ceiling front windows. She said she had some ideas for making some themed pieces that went along with the building and the area, so she was going to get to work on those the very next day.

I was relieved when Shelly agreed to take over my lease from City Market. I would keep some of my photos in that gallery, and she would expand her stained-glass empire, one store at a time. Great friends get a person through hard times, and I was so thankful that Charlie and I had stumbled upon her and Brad that day. It was a random thing, meeting them. Charlie and I had been going for a walk through our neighborhood, when we heard a woman loudly fussing at someone behind a row of tall hedges. As we walked further, we were able to see a short and petite, fiery red-headed woman pointing a finger up at a tall, well-built soldier of a man. Their size difference was hilarious. She was scarcely larger than his thigh, and he could've picked her up with one finger. He had backed over her daylilies while attempting to unload a grill onto the driveway, and she was none too pleased. Charlie volunteered to help him unload, and that was the beginning of a beautiful friendship. God has certainly put us in the right place at the right time, and I don't know what I would've done without them.

By the time I signed the lease for my New York building, I had taken one more personal step. I took my wedding rings off and moved them to the chain that I kept Charlie's rings on. I wore them around my neck daily, a small sign of healing.

I had a month to get things situated before I moved. Packing was the hardest part for me because I felt like I was putting Charlie away. I still had a lot of his clothes and belongings everywhere, untouched since he had gone. I put my most valued mementos and photos from our history in a box labelled "Charlie." His heavy coat hung by the door, and his shoes still sat underneath, on the rug. A handwritten note he had left me on his last morning reminding me that we needed milk, Gatorade, and bananas still hung on the refrigerator.

Our closet was still full of Charlie's clothes. I knew I didn't need to take all of them with me. I went through and kept my favorite shirts and items that he had owned, and I gave Brad the rest to keep or donate as he saw fit. Maybe someone could use them.

The second hardest part was going out into the world to remind *IT* who *I* was. I hadn't had to rely on myself solely, so I made a list of all the major art galleries I could find. I needed to line up some interest and revenue, or I wasn't going to make it. I used the insurance money to pay for my first year's rent in advance, so I would have time to build myself up. I knew, however, that twelve months go by fast.

I had names of galleries and curators from New York, Pennsylvania, New Jersey, Massachusetts, Connecticut, and even Toronto and Montreal. I invested a small fortune into making high-resolution brochures of my best works, along with cover letters, to send out to each and every museum on the East Coast that I could find. "Viral artist, featured in *Arts & Eats* magazine, located in Manhattan's Meatpacking District for the first time!" I used all kinds of blingy words to make myself sound marketable and appealing so that maybe someone would see me, or even better, some newspaper or magazine would see me and write a story about me.

I made sure to include photocopies of my *Arts & Eats* spread, so they'd know I was a legitimate big-time artist, obviously. It was a shot in the dark because I really had no idea how these things are done, and despite my collective experience, I hadn't realized how much I didn't know. Mama always said, "The squeaky wheel gets the grease." I had a lot of squeak and I needed a lot of grease, so I was all in to make the rest of it up as I went along. Fake it til you make it, right?

I needed to form a network of professionals up here in New York, so along with the brochure packets, I included an RSVP for a private showing, curators only. I set the date for two months after I officially moved in, giving myself a full month to get my inventory up, set up a webpage, run marketing, and start attracting local clientele. Roger, who conveniently lived a few streets over, agreed to be cheap labor in exchange for his chance to rub elbows with the art elite. If they showed up, that is.

Roger, Brad, and Shelly all took off five days to help me move and get settled. Shelly and I cleaned all corners of my new living space as well as the gallery while Roger and Brad hung up the chandeliers. They built two display walls, careful to position them for optimal natural lighting. The ceilings on both floors were fourteen feet high, so I had plenty of display space.

Brad and Roger also built a counter space with a wrapping/shipping station, which was a few deep and giant shelves. Shelly and I painted my name and logo on the very back brick wall, behind my counter, so that it was visible from the entrance. I had a professional sign shop make a sign for out front, which was big and grandiose enough to notice, but didn't detract from the scenery of the river and the building itself.

After everything was built, the four of us hurried to get it all painted before Brad and Shelly had to leave. The day before they left, I treated the whole crew to a huge authentic New York Italian dinner for their help. Saying goodbye to Brad and Shelly was bittersweet.

On my first day in my new home, I began unpacking, starting with the "Charlie box." I set some photographs of him at various waterfalls we'd visited in a semi-circle on a side table in the living room. In front of those I placed a border of smooth, multi-colored river stones he had collected over the years. In the middle of the stones, I laid his dried corsage of yellow and orange cornflowers from our wedding. I thought back to all those days we'd spent hiking.

Charlie loved to go hiking, to collect rocks with moss on them, and to collect smooth stones from streams. We shared a mutual love of waterfalls, which we visited frequently. He loved swimming beneath the falls and I loved taking pictures of him as he cannonballed into the frothy water. Another of his favorite hobbies was playing guitar. He had been playing since he was four years old. One of his favorite bands to cover was Coldplay, and he would frequently sing "Green Eyes" to me, saying that it had been written for me all along. I was in love with all of his details.

I had felt full of hope and possibility around him. Charlie was like nothing I had ever known before. With beautiful blue eyes, wavy brown hair and usually a light stubble, he was beautiful without ever having to try. He had a big, wide smile that made his eyes crinkle in the corners. People were naturally drawn to him, and when he laughed the whole room lit up. And somehow, he consistently smelled like apple pie. He made me feel like a better person, more excited and inspired and full of life.

I snapped back into my present world, fully aware that I was completely alone now. I knew no one here except my newly acquired friend, Roger.

Surrounded by the immediate silence, I could only hear the faint wail of sirens in the distance, and the hiss and sizzle of the old coper pipes. I picked up a garbage bag of clothes in my room that I needed to unpack and sat down on the bed. I closed my eyes and took a deep breath before tackling the next suitcase.

I cried myself to sleep each night during my first week alone in New York, weighed down by the new atmosphere around me. The streetlights cast a light yellowish haze through the large windows, and I slept on the couch for a few nights, unable to face a new bedroom with no memories of Charlie in it to keep me company. Part of me felt as if I had betrayed him by leaving him behind. The fact that I was here without my husband, in the future we had so carefully planned, was difficult to believe and accept.

After that first week, I was much more productive. I invested in the best large format giclee printer I could find, which allowed me to print the sharpest images onto canvases to fill my walls. I also had the option of making much smaller canvas prints for tourists and niche collectors within a more modest price point. I tried to cover every angle I could think of to set myself up for success. I also taught myself to make my own frames. Frugal and resourceful, that's how I roll. I spent the next two weeks getting as many of my best photos printed, mounted, and framed as I could. Two unique ideas began to take shape, one on each side of the gallery. One theme would be places and things, and the other would be life and death.

After Charlie died, I had gone back in my grief to Bonaventure, one of the oldest but easily the most beautiful cemeteries in the country. With its huge live oak trees, covered with Spanish moss and sprawling across old dirt paths, its concrete angel statues and meaningful inscriptions on the tombstones, it was easy to be drawn into its shadow and allure.

Sometimes I went on Sundays to sit at the cemetery with Charlie, just to feel close to him. Not many people were there, so I was able to talk to him in peace and not feel judged by watchful eyes. After I had gone several times, I started to notice little subtle things: how the passing clouds affected the shadows, how the moss swayed in the wind, and the way the light fell on the shadows of the angels at the entrance gate, making them look as if they were crying.

I also noticed the seagull that started sitting with me on my balcony. He was missing his right foot and had a heart-shaped scratch on his beak. During my afternoons at the cemetery, I had taken hundreds of photos as a way of dealing with my grief. I hadn't told anyone about these photos at the time. Now, in my New York state of mind and solace, I went through them all for the first time. I chose the ones that spoke to me, and I made sure to leave out the one of Charlie's headstone. I wanted him here with me, but not like that. I wanted to remember him in happier times, and I wanted to be known as more than a widow.

I opened my gallery one month before the RSVP showing, with a lot of help from Roger. He was extremely charismatic and extroverted, and anyone he was acquainted with knew someone who knew someone who knew someone. He had rounded up all his Broadway friends to post or hand out flyers to their important friends and acquaintances. He also advertised for me on his blog, free of charge. I was very hopeful, and a few days after opening, people started arriving.

Surprisingly, I had more than twenty responses from my brochure packets. Many of those were RSVPs from some of the heavy hitters in the curator world. I was impressed with the response because after I had the bright idea to create the packets, my research showed overwhelmingly that it might not have been the best way to go. But I had already spent the money on the brochures, so I decided to chalk it up to a marketing expense for my business and go for it anyway.

Roger helped me start planning the RSVP showing, focusing especially on the appetizers and table setups. He was very excited about finger foods and incorporating some of my Southern traditions, along with his Irish traditions. We ultimately decided on two types of devilled eggs, smoked halibut canapes, and avocado truffles, as well as a few varieties of finger sandwiches. I also purchased champagne to try and impress our guests, which may have been a mistake, since it was one of the less expensive options. I don't drink, so I can't taste the difference. Roger frowned upon tasting it.

"Aye, ye' should've gone fer the Guinness!" he said as he scrunched his nose up and spat out the champagne. Oh well. On the evening of the RSVP showing, Roger and I opted for black tie formal wear. Roger wore a tux and I had chosen a lovely black A-line evening gown, slender against my torso and slightly flowing outward from the waist. It was long enough that I could wear flats, and I always chose comfort over fashion if possible.

I felt excited and dainty, but also uncertain because I hadn't been this person before. I didn't think I looked like the glamourous socialite I was trying to masquerade as. I'm a size ten woman, petite and blonde, with golden ringlet hair. Doll hair. My round face only accents the doll hair effect. I was born with birthmarks in my hair, leaving me with natural white and platinum highlights. Charlie used to say they were marks of greatness. My left eyebrow is half white too, and all my eyelashes on my left eye. My eyes are a light blue to light gray-green, depending on the day and my mood. I thought of myself as more unusual looking than pretty, but Charlie wholeheartedly disagreed.

I usually didn't put a lot of effort into really dressing up. If I had new clothes, that meant they'd been newly added to the clearance racks. I dressed cute, but nothing overly formal. Snazzy for me meant a flowy summer dress. When I was with Charlie, the only formal affairs we were ever invited to were the junior and senior proms, and we had opted to go feed seagulls instead. We valued spending time with each other instead of spending money on fancy clothes. Our wedding had reflected our life together, laid-back and unconcerned with formalities. Now here I was in a classy evening gown living grandly, in my own gallery, in New York. I felt like I was trying to be on a *Vogue* cover, when really I would've been just fine and dandy on a flour sack. I needed a minute to catch my breath.

Roger was the bubblier of the two of us, and clearly used to being the life of the party. When the doors opened at 6:00 p.m., Roger was right there greeting my guests in his cheerful Irish accent. We had a great turnout and made a good chunk of change that night in commissions and sales. Several of the curators told me they would be interested if I photographed certain areas of the city for them, and I struck some deals. Not huge, but also not a bad start for the first month.

Chapter 3

The first six months of business were excellent. In physical sales alone, I made nearly enough to pay a whole year's worth of rent, and in accounts receivable and commissions scheduled on the books, I had enough to live comfortably and put some money in savings. I was also doing pet portraits on select Tuesdays for a fixed price, as some of my cat photos from home had turned out to be immensely popular. That usually brought in enough to pay the utilities alone. I was also careful to unplug my appliances when not in use since a penny saved is a penny earned.

I was busy, so I didn't see Roger much anymore. He was traveling a lot more for his food blog, but we caught up for dinner every few weeks when we were both available. I was still lonely, so I bought a fish. I decided on an orange and white Oscar. They're known to grow huge and can be aggressive with other fish, but they are playful towards their owners. I named him Sid Fishious and put him in a twenty-gallon aquarium. He didn't have a lot of facial expressions, and I felt like it was kind of hard to talk to him and feel as if he genuinely cared. He did let me pet him, so that was something.

After a particularly busy week, not that I was complaining, I decided to close my gallery a little bit early on Friday and take a nap. I had a full day planned on Saturday and some leftover Italian food in the fridge that was calling my name. It was a crisp October day, raining hard outside. I was straightening up in the back when I heard the antique doorbell ring. The time on the clock was 3:04. I looked up but saw no one enter.

I walked over to the left side, the Life and Death gallery, where I saw a man. He was dripping wet and holding a broken umbrella. He was taller than most people, well over six feet. He had golden blonde hair, slicked back, and his skin was pale. He was wearing a three-quarter length tan trench coat and what looked like a three-piece suit underneath that. Quite fancy for an afternoon stroll in the rain, I thought.

I had an extra umbrella that someone had left a few weeks ago during the last storm, I went to fetched it from behind the counter. I went to hand it to the man, but he was not there. I hadn't heard the doorbell, so I walked around to the other side, where I found him staring at one of my photos of a child playing under a bridge.

"May I help you with anything?" I asked. "I have an extra umbrella if you'd like it. I see yours is broken."

The man turned and peered at me. I was standing about four feet away from him, and I could see him clearly now. One raindrop was still clinging to the end of his beautifully proportioned nose. He had ice blue eyes that seemed to pierce into my soul at that moment. He was strikingly, dashingly handsome with slightly pouty, adorable lips. The kind of guy that probably broke a bunch of hearts with those baby blues.

The man had some beard growth, maybe four- or five-days' worth. It was blonde too, so from a distance it had been unnoticeable. He was maybe late thirties or very early forties, and a good foot taller than me I now could tell.

He was the first man I had thought was any sort of attractive since Charlie had passed. We stood there for a few moments staring at each other, probably a full minute in silence at least. I felt awkward in the stillness, but I didn't feel like he was a serial killer searching for his next victim, which is really saying something nowadays. He took the umbrella I offered from my hand, turned, and left. He never uttered a word, strange fellow. I told Sid Fishious about it, but he went on about eating his fish flakes without a care in the world.

The next Friday, the same darn thing happened again. This time it was bright and sunny. I was in the middle of callbacks to let some of my clients know the status of my progress on their commissions when I heard the doorbell ring at 3:04 p.m. on the dot. I finished my phone call and looked up. I couldn't immediately see anyone, so I walked over to the left side, and there he stood. Same tall, beautiful man with the same slicked-back golden hair.

This time I could tell he was in a very well-tailored gray three-piece suit with a light blue shirt and fancy black shoes to finish it off, though I don't know what brand. He was standing there, staring intently at the picture of the seagull with no right foot when I walked up to him.

"Welcome back. How are you today?"

He turned and looked down at me with those ice-blue eyes, more piercing because of his shirt reflecting into them. He handed me the umbrella I had given him and said, "Thank you for letting me borrow this. Good day."

My skin tingled at the sound of his words. He had a deep, slightly raspy purr of a voice. He sounded like a melody, and I noticed a hint of an accent from somewhere I couldn't place. Our overly proper exchange was short, no more, no less. Then he was gone again. Again, Sid Fishious did not care.

The following Friday was a repeat performance. This time I was waiting. Again, it was 3:04 p.m. on the dot when I saw him walk up and open the door. He briskly and quietly walked over to the Life & Death gallery to find me waiting around the corner.

"Hi!" I said.

Startled, the man looked at me like a deer in headlights. He was wearing another three-piece suit, this time darker gray with a light-yellow shirt to accent his golden hair.

"Is there something I can help you with?" I said, slightly pressing. I wasn't afraid of a little confrontation. He stared at me, his cheeks becoming slightly flushed now. "You've been here three weeks in a row, 3:04 p.m. on the dot for the last several weeks, and you've barely spoken to me. Yet you keep coming back and appearing interested in my photographs. I've decided you aren't going to kill me, so I'm going to hold you to that."

He held my gaze for a moment. "Can I take you out for dinner?" My eyes widened in shock.

"Excuse me? No, I do not think that would be appropriate at this time."

I did want to say yes, though. He was extremely attractive. "Forgive me," he said. "My name is Peter Levander. I am the head curator for the photography department at the Metropolitan Museum of Art. You have my word that I will not kill you if you would like to have dinner with me." He grinned slightly, amused at my concern over serial killers.

Man, I didn't see that coming. He knew how to knock a girl off her feet.

I remembered his name from my massive list of brochure packets, but I hadn't received any word from him or the Met.

"The Metro...The Met? The curator? I, um, I didn't—"

"I received your brochure some months ago," he said, still slightly grinning, "when I was out of town attending to family business. By the time I returned, your first showing had already passed. I remembered the perspective you used in your photos and it stuck with me.

"Your Life and Death," he continued, "was not featured in your brochure. What is the reason? It is very striking and became personal to me three weeks ago, as was your kindness. I returned last week, but I still had not reached a final decision, something that does not often elude me. I am here this week to ask if you would like to have dinner with me tonight when your gallery closes."

I was a little flabbergasted at his frankness. He was so proper, so formal. How does one reply? I cleared my throat and stood up straight, my chin slightly higher to match his composure and confidence.

"Yes, that would be a most welcome outing." *A most welcome outing?* Who says that?

"I sense that you are mocking me now."

"I certainly am not. I'm not quite sure how to take you. Dinner at 5:00 will be fine. Shall I meet you out front?"

He grinned and left without another word.

Chapter 4

I closed the gallery about ten minutes early so I could quickly run up and apply fresh deodorant, face powder, and perfume. It's better to be safe than sorry. I was wearing a cute black and white floral blouse and high-waisted gray pants. I felt I looked decently professional enough for an impromptu business meeting. I grabbed a matching coat and headed back down the stairs.

I was super nervous, but I didn't know why. Was it because this man was someone who could advance my career in a hurry? Or was it because he was so adorable? Maybe it was all of the above. I hadn't been on a date, if this was even an official date, since Charlie had died. I had no time to figure it out now, and I rushed back downstairs to hear a strange buzzing sound.

Around the corner came Peter, on a robin's egg blue scooter. He rolled up in front of me. I must've had a very curious expression on my face.

"It is a Honda Metropolitan. She has a few years on her, but highly economical."

"Oh, well, that's fabulously helpful in this bustling city." I was immediately thankful I had pulled my hair back into a ponytail this morning. Peter had somehow found time to change in the last hour, so he must not live too far away. That's the beauty of

New York. It was just like Savannah in that a lot of things are within walking distance.

I was more intrigued by his appearance. He got off the scooter, his frame towering over mine. Gone was the overly professional businessman I had seen up until now. He was wearing a plain white T-shirt, a black leather jacket, dark blue jeans, and black motorcycle boots with his golden, still slicked-back hair. The whole image before me was reminiscent of the 1950s, and I was pleased that my blonde ponytail matched his greaser appearance. He handed me a helmet, and I climbed on behind him. He smelled like a combination of leather and new books, and it was wonderful. Off we scooted.

We went a few blocks over to a quiet little Italian restaurant. This handsome man was confusing. At first, I had thought from his invitation that this was a formal work-related dinner. When he showed up looking so casual, I decided maybe this was an actual date. Now, arriving at this restaurant, I felt like we were formal again. The restaurant was slow, the Friday night rush hour hadn't started yet so we walked right in with no wait. The other patrons were dressed in business and business casual attire. I felt awkward and out of place since this was much fancier than a girl from Georgia was used to. The waiter led us to a more secluded table towards the back, where not so many people were staring at my not-so-fancy appearance.

If I was underdressed, Peter was more so. He removed his leather jacket, revealing his basic white T-shirt. Nothing fancy at all, this was a complete 180 from his visits to the gallery.

"Are we a bit underdressed for this restaurant? I didn't see a dress code when we walked in, but I must tell you I feel very out of place right now."

"No, it is quite all right. I come here all the time, and they know me."

Peter appeared much more relaxed, though still proper. I wondered which was the real Peter. This one, or the serious curator I had seen before? He ordered a glass of wine and a steak, fancy and pricey. Drinking was generally a turn-off for me, but I wasn't sure if this was a date or not. I ordered water and chicken Alfredo, simple and within budget. I had brought my credit card with me, just in case we were going Dutch. A Southern lady is always prepared.

"I have a standing reservation for this table the first three Fridays out of the month," he said. "It's peaceful for me; I like to come where I'm not often bothered by people constantly seeking approval." As he began to feel more at ease around me, his overly proper speech relaxed as well.

His clothing made more sense now. If I didn't know what he did, I'd never be able to tell from the outside. When the waiter had left to put our order in, there was an awkward silence. Peter didn't seem to notice and stared at me, sizing me up with those blue eyes. "Shall we start with the basic Q and A? I'll start since you seem uneasy," he began. "I was born in Gothenburg, Sweden."

Ah, there's the accent. It was so faint it was nearly indistinguishable, but now that I was listening more intently I could pick up on just hint of old-world charm.

"My parents are both teachers, and I have two brothers. I'm the oldest. My middle brother, Mattias, is an artist. He travels a lot between Sweden and Norway for his work. My youngest brother, Caspar, is a thespian. He lives in London's West End right now. He enjoys not knowing where he'll end up, from play to play and year to year. My parents are extremely proud that we have all chosen creative outlets for our occupations."

I took a drink of my water and noticed it had a subtle herb flavor, maybe basil, to heighten the Italian atmosphere. Peter continued, "I enjoy stability and objectivity, and was always more interested in the history of art. I moved from Gothenburg to New York to double major in art history and photography, and I interned at several museums until eventually I worked my way up to my current position. It requires a lot of travel, but I enjoy being based out of New York."

Personal details. Maybe we're on a date after all. I said nothing more about Charlie after telling Peter I was a widow. Stories about Charlie had to be earned. I told him about my hometown, my parents, and my equal passion for art history and photography, which had set me on my journey from a young age.

"My mama handed out photographs of our raggedy, snaggle toothed cat, Stanley like business cards anytime somebody asked about my photography. Before I'd even started high school, I had a large portfolio of portraits and photographs I'd done for all the family and locals. I used that to get my scholarship to SCAD, and the rest is history."

He leaned in closer and asked, "Have any works ever made you cry?"

"Yes, one so far," I said. "When I was in grade school, my mom and I took a weekend trip up to Nashville to the Frist Museum, to see a Degas exhibit. A replica of Degas' *Little Dancer of Fourteen Years* in bronze was featured, and I lost it. To this day, I'm not sure why, but it overwhelmed me. The precision and proportion of it, her proud expression, the history, and the time he spent studying these girls and their movements consumed me. I'm sure if I ever saw the *David* or the *Pietà*, I would do the same or worse—those are on my bucket list." He seemed pleased. "Then that is why you are a photographer. It takes a certain eye to be able to capture detail in the big picture and appreciate art and form. That is a talent I am constantly trying to find. Most think they have the gift, but so few rarely do." *The gift.*

"Photographers can see true, authentic beauty in anything they come across. Beauty, in its purest form, is inspiration enough. That's the gift." My mama used to sing-song those words to me frequently as she rolled biscuits by hand, a cloud of flour around her head as she danced around our kitchen. I felt myself begin to relax. Peter and I seemed to have a lot of things in common. Our food arrived, and the aromas of Italian herbs, cheeses, and chargrilled meats filled the air. "Has any artwork ever made you cry?" I repeated his question back to him. Artistic men are usually more open to their emotions, and I found it a rather endearing trait when men could admit what moved them.

"Yes, two. The first was a photograph, titled *The Vanishing Race* by Edward S. Curtis. I saw it when I was a young child, and I believe that was the moment I knew I was going to be a curator." I had seen the photograph; it was haunting, portraying several Native Americans riding away from the camera on horseback. There was a stark contrast of light and dark, and the more emotional toll was that you knew what they were riding towards, what history had in store for them.

"I wanted to be the one that was responsible for these people, for remembering their fates. For remembering their struggles. That is what moved inside of me and shifted my focus."

Wow, so he's sexy, successful, and a humanitarian, in a sense.

"The second," he continued, "was *The Burning Monk* by Malcolm Browne. It portrays a man's last protest." I heard a quiver in his voice. We ate in silence for a moment.

"That is why I asked you to dinner. Your Life and Death exhibit deeply moves me. I am putting together an exhibition, and I would like to feature several of your photographs, particularly the one of the seagull on the headstone. Capturing expressions on animals is not easy, but I see grief so clearly on his face. Also, I might have a few private collectors who would like to see your photographs." Not a date.

"He's a close friend of mine, and we have a lot of history," I said.

He looked at me strangely.

"I've always connected with animals far better than people, and I do honestly believe they have souls and emotions." Mama always said my photographs were able to capture an animal's soul in their expression.

"Yes, I believe you are right. Most people do not have the gift to capture that on film, so it goes unnoticed in everyday life." The waiter laid the check on the table. I reached down to pull my card from my purse. Peter read my mind and grabbed the check before I could. He handed the waiter a Benjamin, and said, "Keep the change." A date.

"Shall we walk back or scoot?"

I giggled at his playfulness. It was turning a little cold outside, so I opted for the scooter and told him to take me back to the gallery. When we arrived at the gallery, he walked me to the door and said he'd be happy to scoot me to my apartment if I'd let him.

"Well, the thing is, the gallery is my apartment. I don't have any vehicle because my only commute to work is this flight of stairs right here. I'm even more economical than you!"

He flashed a gorgeous smile. Until now, I hadn't yet seen him smile like that. He said, "Touché."

"Thank you for dinner," I said. "It was lovely, and I enjoyed talking to you. I trust I'll be hearing from you when you're closer to setting up your exhibition?" I was going to be nonchalant and not set myself up for failure in case he wasn't romantically interested in me.

"Thank you for a lovely evening. I quite enjoyed your company and conversation; it's not often that I get to connect with someone on shared interests. You might think otherwise considering my occupation, but usually I get trapped into endless conversations with people who are trying to convince me how relevant their works are to the world. Do you own a ball gown?"

I stood there silently for a few seconds. Peter had thrown me off guard again.

"I own a gown. It's not a ball gown, but it's kind of swanky, I guess." The only fancy dress I owned was the one I had worn at my RSVP showing.

"Would you like to go ballroom dancing with me next Friday night? On the fourth Friday of the month, I take a ballroom class. It starts at 6:00, and we can get dinner after." A date.

"That sounds like so much fun, but I can't dance."

"That's alright. I can teach you. The basics are easy, and from there, you build up. The class is full of beginners, so you won't feel out of place at all. You have my word. I will pick you up at 5:30?" I couldn't very well say no to that.

He shook my hand, climbed back onto his scooter, and drove away.

The next day was the first time that I did not wear my wedding rings in some form since Charlie had passed. I took off the necklace containing them and placed it in my jewelry box. As much as it pained me, I felt as though maybe it was time to start looking ahead. I knew Charlie would want me to move on, but part of me still felt so weird, being here and doing all of this without him.

A few hours later, I was sitting out on my balcony eating a biscuit and reading the latest *National Geographic*, when I heard a flutter on the opposite end of me. I peered over my magazine, and I saw my seagull, missing his right foot and sporting a heart-shaped scratch on his beak. I had not seen him in a few months, not since business had started taking off. I was surprised he was still here, and I certainly didn't think he ever would've followed me from Savannah. But here we were, me and Major Birdie Biddle eating biscuits in New York.

It was such a comfort to see him, and in my heart, I believed it was Charlie watching out for me all this time, letting me know everything was okay. "Hey, Major Biddle!" I threw part of my biscuit a few feet away from me, and he flew down off the railing and hopped over to eat it.

Chapter 5

I didn't hear from Peter all week. I called Shelly and told her all about it so we could analyze each little detail together, but she was as confused as I was. We decided that our first dinner was definitely not a date but more of a professional courtesy type of dinner. It was an "I like your work; I'm going to buy you dinner and persuade you to work with me, and we will both profit from it" dinner.

The jury was still out on ballroom dancing. Shelly said Brad had never taken her ballroom dancing, ever. That's not even a thing that people did in Savannah, at least that we knew of. We decided this was one of those city boy foreign subjects we would have to learn about before we could determine if it was a real date.

By Wednesday, I had almost convinced myself it was a complete fantasy that I had hallucinated because none of it seemed real. He was too gorgeous, he smelled too good, and the whole ambiance of the evening was too mesmerizing.

Fridays tended to be slow when the weather was cold. I took the opportunity to wash my hair early that morning. I rolled it up with clips and a few strategically placed rollers so that when my blonde curls dried, they would look like voluminous, glamorous Hollywood starlet hair.

My naturally curly hair helped to maintain volume if I could get it to dry just right, and if this wasn't a date, I was still going out with a bang. I wrapped a scarf around my rollers so that if anyone walked in, they wouldn't be able to see the conundrum atop my head. I closed the gallery at 4:30 so I could have enough time to change and let my hair down. I was even more nervous about this night than the last because now I was going into unchartered territory. I was great at eating dinner, a pro I would say, but I had no clue about ballroom dancing.

My hair method did not disappoint. As I let my curls down, they fell luxuriously around my face and down my neck. I put on makeup, just enough to match my hair but not so much that I didn't still look somewhat natural. "Enhanced natural," Mama said. The beauty of wearing black was it provided a blank slate so I could accent my eyes according to my mood. I opted for green tonight, to counter Peter's intense blue eyes. I also added a hint of black liner, with a splash of some dark and light purple shades.

I stained my lips light pink, again not dark enough to be noticeable, but just enough to enhance my natural pink. My dress was comfortable enough that I thought it might make a good dancing dress. We were about to find out.

Instead of wearing my usual flats, I decided to wear some black strappy heels. They were comfortable enough to walk in, and I had worn them with jeans frequently throughout the years when I wanted to show off a pedicure and add some flair to my look.

The final touch was a spritz of Jessica McClintock perfume divided between my wrists and neck for a floral and flirty mood. The last week of October had turned out to have colder nights, so I put on a fitted coat just in case. By then, it was almost time. I locked up and headed back downstairs. Peter was waiting for me outside the gallery door. He was dressed head to toe in a tuxedo, his golden hair slicked back as usual. He had also shaved, which looked just as good on him as not. I was pleased that all my efforts matched him. We looked pretty darn cute if I do say so myself, like Ballroom Barbie and Ken. He stared at me for a minute, his beautiful lips slightly open. He looked as if he were about to say something but changed his mind.

"What, no scooter tonight?" I said with a slight smile, tilting my head to the side, eyebrows raised.

Peter smiled back. "No, I thought we could just walk if that would be all right. It is two blocks north of here. I live two blocks east of here, if you were wondering. That Italian place we went to last week, I can see it from my apartment. I usually only use my scooter for going to work. It cuts down on the traffic and only takes me about twenty minutes." His gaze met mine as he finally said the compliment he had probably meant to start with: "You look astonishing."

I felt myself blush as I looked away. I was glad I decided to wear walking heels instead of something impractical. I wouldn't have to look like an idiot going back up to change shoes.

Along our stroll to the class, we talked about the weather, politics, this and that, and nothing in particular. He had been in a gallery in New Jersey for several days this week, arranging exhibitions, surveying their inventory, doing all the things curators did. As we walked along the street overlooking the Hudson River, the sun started to set, and a romantic orange light cast over us.

We walked for a minute more, then went in an unassuming looking building. It looked like an abandoned department store on the outside, looming and dark as we walked up. It smelled musty and initially looked even older than my building with tin ceilings and copper pipes. The lighting was dim at the entrance, but as we walked in, the tone changed. The room turned into an art deco ballroom from the 1920s, and I felt as though I had arrived in West Egg.

Music played in the background, somehow classic and modern at the same time. Old wooden panels on the walls and gold fixtures lined the main lobby. Old fashioned benches with golden feet lined each side, with marble-topped side tables in between them. At any moment someone might greet us with a cigar and a glass of brandy as we stood at the door. We fit in perfectly with our surroundings, and I took a moment to be proud of myself for picking such a great all occasion dress. I noticed a few older women were standing around talking, in beaded dresses of all lengths, each style resembling a flapper dress.

They came up to talk to Peter, and he stepped a foot or two away from me for just a moment. Uncomfortable in my skin, I did a little jig to the music. I didn't think anyone saw me until I glanced up. Peter had turned back around, and he was paying attention. With an amused smile on his face, he took my hand and led me into a grand ballroom. An enormous crystal chandelier hung in the center of a brightly lit room. The wall was lined with mirrors from floor to ceiling, and to my right, the wall was lined with chairs, filled with older men and women in various era dresses and tuxedos.

In the back corner was a water table, surrounded by people in all sorts of outfits, and in the front corner was a table with an old record player on it. Dressed in a long-tailed tuxedo and top hat, a man stood beside it, whom I assumed was the DJ, and was organizing the records. He looked exactly like the Monopoly man, but without a spectacle.

"The regulars take their wardrobes seriously here," Peter said. "A lot of these people were actors and actresses at some point in their life, so they go all out to try and outdo each other. They pay no attention to newcomers; their only rivalries are amongst each other. Just ask any of them to fill you in on all the latest gossip between them. They out-dance and out-dress each other here, but then tomorrow they'll have a big book club meeting at a restaurant of their choosing. They've stayed together as a tight-knit community throughout the years."

Peter pointed out the other groups to me as well. "The group over in the corner by the water table are newer attendees. They're of various ages and professions, and they were all invited here by some of the veteran dancers. One or two of them have grandmas in that group we passed outside."

He continued, taking careful consideration to provide full descriptions and details of all the groups so I wouldn't feel out of place. "Over there in the opposite corner is the Charleston group. They have danced for years together. Most of them are retired from Broadway, and they go on trips to anywhere you could imagine. They recently returned from a week in Vermont. They said it was a little too cold, but they will try again next year in early fall right as the leaves start to turn. At the end of our class, they'll come in and do their big number. They take it seriously and are fiercely coordinated."

He came to the last group. "That group in the middle is the veteran students and teachers. They're doing their stretches and warm-ups right now. My neighbor is one of them. She is how I found out about this class. She offered free lessons if I agreed to dance with a lot of the older women who didn't have partners. I enjoyed it so much I kept coming back."

Then I heard a familiar Irish voice approach me from behind.

"Well, the mystery man finally brought a date—Hey! Cecelia! How are ye?"

Roger gave me a huge scooping hug. I hadn't seen him in about two months. He'd been traveling around the East Coast for his blog. Ashamedly, during the times he'd been so sweet to help me out, I hadn't asked too much about his personal life other than the basics. I was so preoccupied with trying to get my life up and running that I had no clue that he took ballroom lessons. It made complete sense, with all the other Broadway people here letting loose.

"How d'ye manage to catch him? He's as elusive as they come," he said in his sing-song voice as he gave Peter the once-over. I was more accustomed to his accent by now, but my ears were still slow to pick a few words.

"Peter was planning to come to my RSVP showing, but he had to be out of town. He came by to see the gallery as soon as he could, and now here we are!"

They shook hands, and Roger said with an amused expression, "Aye then, I'll let ye get back to it, but I'll steal her away later for a few dances!" And he skipped off to stir up some of the wallflowers.

The lights flickered the five-minute warning, and Peter took my hand and pulled me aside to teach me the basics. He gently placed his right hand on my waist, which I liked the feeling of, and put my left hand on his shoulder. He took my right hand in his left and outstretched them together.

"This is your basic frame. From here, you can control me, and I can control you." He moved our hands loosely around. "Do not let me move your hand; that is breaking frame. Stay strong against my movements. When I push, you push back, and we maintain control together. When I step forward, you mirror my foot movements. You will feel the front of my thighs on yours, pushing yours back until you get comfortable enough, and then you'll automatically move on your own. Don't just move your feet. Shift your weight or you'll get lost in the steps. Or worse, I will step on you."

We both laughed, and I could feel my face was bright red from nerves and from being so close to this gorgeous man.

"We'll start off slow," he said, still holding me, "but then we'll have to pick up the pace, or people will run over us. I will be leading you, so you will be dancing backward as I dance forward. We'll be going in a giant circle with everyone else, but you cannot focus on what they're doing. Watch me and trust that I will not run you into anyone." The scent of his cologne, coupled with our bodies locked in frame, made me weak in the knees.

I was exhilarated and terrified at the same time, and excited to be learning something new, even if I was about to make a fool of myself in front of all these career dancers. Go big or go home, right? That was my new motto, and well, I had great hair, so I was staying out tonight!

When the music finally started, it was a slow, modern romance song that I faintly recognized but could not place. Peter swept me onto the dance floor, our eyes locking for a few minutes. I do this thing where I have this big stupid grin on my face when I'm nervous and concentrating at the same time, so I'm sure I looked totally awesome right then.

"You're staring," he said in a soft purr.

"I'm sorry. I'm trying to concentrate," I said as I almost fell over from Peter distracting my focus. He smiled at me sweetly as we continued to twirl about the floor.

"Remember to shift your weight. Don't just move your feet."

No, I had already forgotten to do that, but I started doing it, and the steps improved tenfold. I thought back to all the *Dancing with the Stars* episodes I had watched and wondered how long it took them to develop muscle memory.

After I was confidently dancing backward through the first few waltzes, the pace quickened. Roger appeared out of thin air to steal me away, and Peter excused himself to go dance with some of the older women. I noticed it was much easier dancing with Roger because neither of us was worried about the fact that we looked like two idiots twirling around.

"But seriously, how d'ye catch him?" Roger asked. "He's not brought a single soul here. Two years he's been dancin'! I've been comin' fer tree!"

Tree? My brain quickly translated his accent again and realized he had said, "three."

I shrugged as we danced. "I'm not sure, honestly. Peter has been coming to the gallery a lot to look at the Life and Death exhibit. We went out to dinner last week, now here we are this week, and that's all I know."

"Aye, he was comin' to the gallery to look at ye' I suspect." We both giggled. "You'd better watch out, or she'll get at ye'. She's been after him, and he hasn't given her the time o' day."

"Who?"

Right then, as if on cue, a woman about my age with dark brunette hair and glasses bumped Roger out of the way and replaced his frame. Roger winked at me before disappearing into the circle of dancers.

"Hi there, I'm Tara. You're new here. I saw you walk in with Peter. How did the two of you meet?"

She was pushy. I sensed that she was trying to be the alpha female, but I'm Southern and slightly taller. I pushed back.

"Hi, I'm Cecelia. You must be the neighbor. I met Peter through work. He visits my gallery frequently. He asked if I wanted to come tonight, and here we are."

"Hmmm. Well, he's a good guy. He mentioned me?"

"No. He never mentioned you before tonight, and when we arrived, he didn't mention you by name, only that you had given him free lessons. I put two and two together when you cut in just now." She looked aggravated, but I used my height difference to stare her down to size.

Then Roger found his way back to me and cut back in. Tara didn't say another word as she disappeared into the swirling crowd. "She looked rightly perturbed. What d'ye say to her? I didn't take ye for the aggressive type."

"I politely put her in her place is all. She was in my territory." We laughed and twirled and laughed some more. The music switched to a faster song that I couldn't keep up with, so Roger and I retired to the water table, where Peter was waiting for me.

"Get a tall drink of water from a tall drink of water," Roger teasingly whispered in my ear as we walked up, and I blushed dark red.

Peter handed me a cup and said, "Are you enjoying the evening?"

"Yes, thank you. More than I thought I would."

We stood there for a minute. I hadn't realized how out of breath I was until I stopped moving. Peter watched me with a tender expression.

"I think you'll like the Charleston ladies. They will be doing their routine when the next song plays. After that, if you would like to leave, there is a wonderful Greek place around the corner."

"Oh! That sounds wonderful! I was so focused on making the right movements that I forgot to be hungry, but my stomach is growling."

The lights flickered and after a minute were lowered. A disco ball came out, and a spotlight pointed to the middle of the room. The music started, at first just a drum beat and then full-on brass and the works. I immediately recognized it as a song from the Big Band era, but I couldn't recall the name. Then the Charleston ladies began the dance for which they were named, perfectly synchronized with their arms and legs flailing about in coordinated chaos. Not missing a beat, step, or kick, they were quite stunning, seeming to have more fun than I'd seen anyone have in a long time.

When their performance was over, the crowd erupted into applause and shouting, and Peter took my hand. I waved goodbye to Roger, and Peter guided me around the edge of the room to the door. We passed by Tara, who stared me down with an icy chill. Not bothered at all, I smiled and waved at her.

As the evening began to wind down, several people in the lobby called out to Peter, who smiled and waved to them as we walked out, still holding hands. When we were outside, I let go of his hand. My adrenaline was so pumped up I wasn't even cold, so I tied my coat around my waist. I was practically jumping up and down I was so excited. Peter laughed at me.

"So, you had fun?" he asked.

"Are you kidding me? That last number was incredible! I have to learn the Charleston now." I stopped on the sidewalk, under a lamppost, and tried to mimic what I'd seen. "It's amazing! It was all amazing! The outfits, the lighting, the music, the people—all of it was like being in a movie. It was awesome!"

I looked up at him, a sparkle in my eyes. He wrapped his arms around my waist right then and kissed me, so light yet so certain. Surprised, I caught my breath and threw my arms around his neck and kissed him back. Definitely a date.

Chapter 6

From then on, whenever Peter was in town, Friday night dates were a standing arrangement. I only ever saw him on Friday evenings. If I did see him any times outside of that, they were few and far between, usually when he was bringing a client by my gallery. Time with him felt limited and scheduled, which was perfect for me in a way.

Occasionally we would go to another part of the city, but for the most part, we were very routine. He'd pick me up at 5:00 p.m. on Fridays, and we'd eat Italian the first three Fridays, followed by one or two foreign movies. Fourth Friday dance class was a standing arrangement as well, and I invested in several more dresses to mix it up.

On movie nights, we would go out to dinner and either go to the cinema to watch the latest foreign film or walk back to either his apartment or mine to watch whichever film he had newly acquired. My favorite movies were the Italian ones, and I had since taken up learning Italian in my free time. It was such a beautiful language, and I loved the excitement for life that the language and the movies portrayed. I had always had a secret passion for Italian opera, but no one ever shared it, so I kept it to myself mostly.

Peter's obvious favorites were the Swedish movies, which were not at all foreign to him, of course. I tried to learn the language, but the pronunciation is a lot different from English, Spanish, or Italian. Spanish was easy for me to pick up since as an American I was already so used to it. I couldn't speak it well, but I could read it and understand the gist of someone else saying it.

Swedish was different, and much harder for me to wrap my brain around. I tried for several weeks to learn Swedish for him, but usually I'd end up making him laugh hysterically at my failures to construct sentences and proper phrasing. I didn't mind, because Peter's ice-blue eyes were dazzling when he laughed.

"Just say it one more time, for me."

"Whalepeddle." Peter doubled over in laughter as I hopelessly failed to say the Swedish word for turtle.

Peter maintained his mysterious charm. He was wonderful when he let loose—fun and charming and charismatic—but that side of him rarely made an appearance. He kept some walls up, which I felt like I couldn't break through. I think he let me in closer than most people, but I didn't feel like we were quite connected.

I did consider him my very best friend, and on rare occasions he would break routine and take me to parties or dinners with his colleagues when he had the opportunity. But I didn't feel as if I fit in with that crowd. Maybe that was why he liked me so much.

I felt awkward in these situations, and I said the wrong things. His colleagues seemed more educated than me, a different pedigree altogether. I felt like they looked down at me and my Southern accent, even though I could easily hold my own with them, given my résumé and accolades.

Peter didn't seem to notice, or if he did, he didn't let it phase him. He said I reminded him of his home, of being comfortable and at ease. We seemed to have just about everything in common, but the atmosphere between us generally felt a little peculiar. We never spent the night together or engaged in anything physical other than kissing. He didn't ask, nor did I offer; I wasn't that type of woman.

We didn't talk about the future, in a relationship sense of being. He didn't introduce me as his girlfriend, either. I obviously was, and he obviously talked about me quite a bit to those around him, but we didn't declare the formal titles. I thought that was odd. Charlie had been adamant about letting me know how he'd felt from the beginning.

What seemed like Peter's mysterious charm the first few months grew tiresome after a while, because I had no clue how he felt about me. Not really. Part of me was fine with things as they were, because I still missed Charlie. I still thought about him a lot, and I talked to Peter about him occasionally. I decided Peter meant to give me enough space without pressure.

We loved each other, I knew that much, but I was not in love with him. Maybe if we were together longer, once I'd fully healed, we would fall in love? I knew eventually I would want more, a relationship full of time together and not weekly pre-arrangements. I had no definite reason for not being in love with Peter. He was supportive, kind, caring, sweet, successful, and handsome as all get out. If he was in love with me, he never said as much, or mentioned it at all.

On one Friday, seven months into our relationship, we watched *Cinema Paradiso*, one of my favorites of the Italian movies we'd seen. When it ended, I got up to get some juice. Peter followed me into the kitchen and started kissing my neck. He was a fantastic kisser, and I loved the way his lips felt against mine. I turned around to kiss him back, and he undid the top button of my blouse. I put my hands up and pushed his hands away, still kissing him. He reached up and undid my second button. I wanted to do more, I did. I longed for the touch of a man again, but I was not in love with Peter. I was not going to sleep with someone, even my best friend, if we were not married and thus fully committed to each other.

I thought then of Charlie, of how we had saved ourselves for our wedding night, and of all the firsts I had had with him. I started sobbing. Peter stopped kissing me and instead held me tightly, securely in his arms.

"I am sorry, Cecelia. I wasn't trying to push you," he said.

"I'm sorry too. I can't. That's not who I am."

Peter walked me home, and we were silent all the way. When we arrived at my gallery, he stopped and turned to me. He kissed me in his sweet way and said, "In two weeks, I have to go home to Sweden for a few days for work. I only found out today, or I would have told you sooner. I'd like you to come with me if you can. I think it would be great for you to get away and see some sights, maybe take your camera and do some exploring." We booked our tickets the next day.

Chapter 7

It was the first week of June, and the weather was a perfect seventy degrees in New York City. The sun was out, the birds were singing loudly, and I was about to be a globetrotter. I had never been out of the country, so to say I was excited was an understatement, and I made sure to pack extra rolls of film. I also packed some additional layers of clothing for my trip just in case, since I wasn't too confident about how warm Sweden was in the spring. To stay true to our economical selves, we booked the cheapest seats available last minute, which was still more than I would've normally paid. I'm a fan of planning things as soon as possible. The early bird gets the fattest, cheapest worms that way.

We flew out of LaGuardia in coach, and were soon in our first of two layover cities, Toronto. After we boarded our next plane to Frankfurt, I hoped to snag a nice eight-hour nap. The few places Charlie and I had ever flown hadn't been far enough away to even warrant a nap in the first place. I decided now would be a great time to try. I asked the flight attendant for an extra blanket and pillow. I reclined my seat the whole two inches it would go and tucked myself in as best I could.

I hadn't dreamed about Charlie in a long time, not since dating Peter that I could remember. Peter, even in all his mystery, had helped to heal my heart and my mind, and I was eternally grateful to him for that.

I was feeling like I had been in a deep sleep for hours when I started dreaming about Charlie. I was so happy to see him, to be with him after so long. We were walking along the top edge of a waterfall, no, of waterfalls! I saw at least six of them, maybe more, and the air temperature was so cold I had to put my hands on my nose to warm it up. The cascades were beautiful, unlike anything I'd ever seen before.

I knew we were too close to the side, and I didn't even want to look over for fear of falling. Charlie was walking beside me on my right, towards the land, and I was towards the edge. His position struck me as odd. Charlie knew I had vertigo, and he was always one for chivalry. He wouldn't have put me this close to danger on purpose.

I started to ask how'd he'd been. I paused. A strange melody was drifting across the waterfalls. As I listened closely, I could hear the music more clearly now. A quieter piano melody, it sounded classical and well-known, but I couldn't place it. The tones were haunting and sad, dramatic and powerful. The emotion of the moment washed over me, and I wanted to cry from the sensations I was feeling. I looked over at Charlie, who had stopped walking and was standing there smiling at me.

"What is this music?" I said. My back was to the waterfalls as Charlie said nothing, smiling at me with those crinkles in the corners of his eyes.

"Why aren't you talking? Charlie?"

He hugged me, kissed my cheek, and let me go. He didn't push me, but he didn't try to steady me as I lost my footing and slipped. I could still see him smiling as I fell backward over the edge.

I awoke with a start, my hands grasping the arms of my chair as the plane hit heavy turbulence again. Peter jolted upright also. He had fallen asleep on my shoulder, so I had unknowingly given him midair whiplash.

"Are you okay? What happened?" he said.

With tears in my eyes, I was breathing hard as I shook my head and said, "It's nothing. I had a bad dream is all." He kissed my forehead and signaled the stewardess to bring me a ginger ale.

When we arrived in Frankfurt, we had about two hours until our next flight landed, so I grabbed us a bite to eat. I felt as if the only logical choice to make was bratwurst and strudel from one of the vendor carts, and then I found a nice, open table away from the crowds. Peter was on his phone as soon as we landed, talking furiously in Swedish and pacing back and forth around the table.

My Swedish was extremely shoddy. I had only managed to learn a few basic phrases such as *ursäkta* (I'm sorry), *tack så mycket* (Thank you so much), and a few various other words. Now, I was trying desperately but failing to understand Peter in his native tongue. The only thing I was able to pick up on was *Svenska,* Sweden, so something definitely was happening in Sweden. Or something was not happening in Sweden.

My mind was playing out a thousand different scenarios as I chowed down on my delicious bratwurst, juice dripping down my hands. Peter hung up the phone aggressively, and I could only think back to when wall phones still existed. The only sheer pleasure of having a wall phone had been slamming it down in disgust whenever the situation arose.

As I watched Peter pacing back and forth behind my bratwurst, he stopped and tapped his phone so hard that the other person surely felt it on the other line. He then made another phone call, again in Swedish, but this time much more civil. I heard my name mentioned, and I wished I would've paid more attention to those Swedish movies and tried to learn more from the subtitles. As I bit into my apple strudel, buttery pastry goodness filled my mouth. I closed my eyes to savor the flavor, humming and smiling to myself in the process.

When I opened my eyes, Peter was sitting in front of me, a pinched expression on his face. I could tell he was annoyed. "Is everything okay?" I said.

"No, it is not okay. I want to apologize to you, Cecelia. I have tried and failed to rearrange things on your behalf." Now I was really worried.

"A few days ago, before we left, I heard that I did not need to be in Gothenburg for work. Instead, the museum needed me to travel to Copenhagen to a large showing there."

Um, no. That's not the plan.

"That was not the plan we had made. I informed the museum that I would be bringing a guest as well, so I needed to know more accurate details, before I rearranged your flights and plans. I heard nothing, so I assumed our plans were a go. They were not. I must be in Copenhagen, Denmark, tomorrow."

"What? But I don't have a plane ticket! Can we get a plane ticket in time? I can't speak Swedish, let alone stay by myself!" My voice was getting squeakier the more worried I became.

"Do not worry. It's handled. With work changing my itinerary, I will not have much time to spend with you if I take you to Copenhagen. I have arranged for you to stay with my brother, Mattias. He's in Gothenburg this week. We were going to stay with him anyway, so now it will just be you. I called him a few minutes ago, and he is aware of the situation. He's more than willing to be your tour guide for the next several days. Your visit will be a good change for him as well.

I will be escorting you to my parents' house to see you off, and then I will have to come back to the airport to catch my next flight. That is the only arrangement I could get the museum to do for me. From there, you will be with him until I return to you."

I sat there for a second, dumbfounded. I was no longer in the mood to finish my strudel, which was a real tragedy. I was so angry at him, but there was nothing he or I could've done to fix it.

"So, you're dumping me off on your brother, who I haven't met, for a week and forcing him to do all the touristy things with me that you were going to show me? Can he even speak English!?" My voice was almost to shrieking level.

Peter chuckled, "Yes, he can speak English. A lot of Swedes can. Cecelia, I am truly sorry. I tried to fix this situation, but this is the best they could do. I must represent the museum in Copenhagen. I am the only curator who is already so close to the area, so they saw a great opportunity. It wouldn't have been a problem had I not had company." Not the best thing to say at the moment.

"Wouldn't have been a problem? Well, I'm sorry I'm such a problem for you then."

"That's not what I meant, and you know it. Please don't be upset and make this a big deal. It will be fun for you, and great for my brother. He could really use the company. He has had a lot going on and needs a welcome distraction. He's more than happy to escort a beautiful American woman around our native country."

I huffed for a minute as he started in on his bratwurst.

"Nothing sounds bad when you say it like that. I'm still going to be upset, but I guess it'll be fine."

He smiled and then finished off the strudel.

Chapter 8

We arrived in Gothenburg in the early morning hours. The surroundings outside the airport had a faint gray-orange glow from the sunrise coming through the many clouds. I couldn't tell if it would rain or not, it wasn't quite bright enough to distinguish the clouds yet. I could feel that the air was different here, much different from New York. It was light and crisp, and it raced through my nostrils like the sensation I get from peppermint gum. We took an Uber to a suburb lined with townhomes along both sides of the streets. The neighborhood was a very clean and average looking area. It reminded me of the quaint little street in Savannah where my apartment with Charlie was, so already I felt comfortable in strange surroundings.

The car stopped at a charming townhome with flowerbeds on either side of the doorway. In them were adorable little flowers, which Peter called "twin flowers." They looked like they were wildflowers, with two little pastel pink bells hanging atop a skinny stem. I noticed the beds were not made of traditional dirt but had what looked like a lot of moss and peat to give it a woodsier effect.

Peter said the twin flowers were native to the more Northern regions of Sweden, but his mother loved them so much that his father had tried to recreate their preferred habitat so she could see them every day. I knew I was going to like his parents already. Peter asked the driver to wait a moment, and we stepped out of the car and walked to the front door.

After Peter unlocked it, we entered a dark, freezing hallway. I noticed a small shelf inside the door as Peter took his shoes off and placed them on it. "You should do the same," he said, nodding towards the shelf. "It is customary in Sweden."

Beneath us were old wooden floors that looked as if they had been freshly polished. As my feet touched the wood, I realized how thin my socks were. I didn't remove my coat.

"Let me give you a quick tour," Peter said as I glanced around. Family photos hung on either side of the somewhat faded floral wallpaper. I could tell it had been a vibrant cerulean blue background with small thin vines running vertically.

"My parents are both teachers at the university, so they will be back later this evening. They know you are here, and are excited to meet you if time permits, so please do not feel like you are intruding. Mattias is supposed to be here already. I can only stay for twenty minutes before I have to go. My next flight is in two hours." He called out his brother's name. Silence. He walked upstairs and called again to more silence.

I started to panic. What if Mattias didn't show? What if he thought it was next week? A thousand new scenarios set in, which Peter read on my face.

"Do not worry. I'll stay with you a few minutes more and then I'll call him on my way back to the airport. He is quite dependable. Our family prides itself on being reliable."

"That's funny since that's how I got into this situation." He looked at me, and I could tell he was slightly hurt.

"I'm sorry, Peter, *ursäkta*. I'm stressed out right now in a foreign country with the one person I know leaving me in a few minutes. I won't be mad once my stress level returns to normal."

He smiled and gave me a quick rundown of the house, telling me I was welcome to whatever I wanted in the kitchen if I were hungry. I walked him to the door and he leaned in. Slowly and apologetically he kissed me. He pulled away, his lips lingering just a breath from mine. Then he was gone.

I walked back into the kitchen, which was adorable. It reminded me of my kitchen back in New York. Shiny copper pans hung on a shiny copper pot rack over a white marble island. Lining the walls behind the oven and sink were white and pistachio tiles. Above the sink was a window overlooking the backyard, and beside the old-fashioned-looking refrigerator was the back door.

I walked outside, taking pictures of the various flowers and plants. I saw an old wooden swing stationed towards the back. It had so many vines growing up and around it that it looked more natural and fairylike than man-made.

I went back inside after a few minutes, the low growl from my stomach guiding me. I looked through the refrigerator and chose some juice to keep me company. I walked back into the hallway, towards the front. The living room was on the righthand side after the foyer, and I wandered from wall to wall, looking at all the family's pictures of selected moments from their accomplishments, lives and travels.

Master's degrees, theatre degrees, and art degrees were all showcased alongside pictures of safaris, oceans, landscapes, famous buildings, and landmarks. A photo of an adorable blonde couple, who must be Peter's parents, sitting in the backyard swing caught my eye. The vines wrapped around the swing were full of blooms, and she was smelling a bouquet of twinflowers as he kissed her forehead. Above the mantel hung a beautiful oil painting on canvas that I recognized as the Northern Lights.

Just then, I heard music coming from another room. It grew louder in the silence, and I realized maybe it had been quietly playing all along, though I wasn't sure. I turned to follow the sound, a faint piano melody I could hear a little more clearly now. As I drifted up the stairs, I realized I had heard it before but I didn't know from where.

When I reached the top of the stairs, the haunting melody now sounded as if it were coming from the back corner. I walked towards it and entered the dark room, a bedroom of a boy, a teenager, or a man. Stacks of books and rolled maps and rolled canvases lined the dark navy-blue walls. The music drew me closer.

Light streamed from a small bedroom window, and as I walked over to it I saw it was overlooking the area of backyard where I had just been. A record player was sitting on a table a few feet away, the sound of the piano hauntingly echoing in my presence. The record was unmarked, but as I stood there, I realized where I'd heard it before. It was the same unforgettable melody from my last dream about Charlie, the one with the waterfalls. Tears filled my eyes, and I turned the sound up, lost in the emotion of the music.

I don't know how long I stood there. I heard a sound behind me that brought me out of the haze of grief. I turned around to face the doorway, tears still welled in my eyes. Leaning against the doorframe a few feet away, silently observing me, was a man. He looked out of place, as if he had wandered in off the street, but I was not afraid of him. He was wearing ragged old jeans and an old long-sleeved brown shirt with paint stains on it. He barely resembled Peter at all. He was tall, about the same height as Peter. He looked older, as if he had had a rough few years, but I knew he was younger.

Weathered and worn down, this was a man who had already hit rock bottom and was now hovering a few inches above it. He had the same broad shoulders, but he was skinnier and wirier than Peter, and his cheeks were slightly gaunt. Where Peter's nose,

73

chin and overall face were more rounded, this man's features were somewhat more angled and pointed. Instead of Peter's golden locks, he had dark brown and thinning hair, and a stringy, unkempt beard of several weeks.

Despite his enervated appearance, he was savagely handsome. He had a pained, wistful look in his eyes, but at the same time I could tell they were still wild and fierce like a lion. They were a much deeper blue than Peter's, more somber and tranquil in color.

He stood up straight when he saw I'd noticed him, and I could smell the vodka permeating from him. We made eye contact and stood there, watching each other for a few seconds. "What is this music?" I said.

"I wrote it. For my son," he said.

I stood there, dumbfounded. "Has it ever been published?"

"No, no one else has ever heard it except for you. Just now. I only write music for myself."

He looked even sadder as he said it.

"You must be Cecelia. I'm Mattias. I am sorry, I didn't hear you come in. I was up in the attic when you arrived. Peter called me just now to tell me you were here, and that he'd arrived back at the airport."

He walked up to me and shook my hand. The moment our skin touched, I felt intensely at ease with this total stranger who was responsible for me over the next several days.

"Peter said you're a painter, which you obviously are by your outfit. You compose too?"

"I've done a little bit of everything. When I was a child, I took ballet, various other dance classes, and music classes. When I was a teenager, I did sculpture and cinematography. Now I'm a painter. I have only composed a handful of works." I noticed his voice was lighter than Peter's in tone, and he didn't try to be as stiff and proper with his words. Where Peter usually spoke in a low purr, Mattias spoke in a whimsical manner, like a windchime, that made me hang on each word with fascination.

"That's amazing. How is it possible that you've done all of that?"

"You mean to say, why do I get bored so easy? That's what people mean to say, only not so polite as you. The world is rich in experiences, and I believe that one should try to experience as many of them as possible. People shouldn't get themselves stuck in the mundane of the ordinary. That is how people lose their minds." His expression was a million miles away, but then he was quickly back in front of me and smiling.

"But don't try to fool me, I heard your stomach growling over the music, so let me get changed and then we'll go eat."

When Mattias returned, he had changed into a navy-blue V-neck sweater, accenting his deep blue eyes even more, and newer, much nicer jeans. He picked up my purple suitcase with sea turtles on it and carried it outside to a silver Volvo XC40. I hadn't noticed a car when Peter and I had arrived, but here it was, now with my suitcase going into its hatchback trunk.

"Are you able to drive?" I asked, still smelling the faint lingering of vodka.

"Yes, I don't drink anymore if that is what you are referring to, and I've quite a built-in tolerance so that you wouldn't even be able to recognize if I was impaired."

I laughed nervously. "How long has it been since you quit drinking?" I asked, half curious and half mocking.

"Almost an hour now." He looked at me with a half-grin and a glint in his wild eyes. My mouth fell open slightly as I stared at him. I couldn't read him well enough to know if he was joking or not, and I knew almost nothing about his character. Peter didn't speak of him much.

Mattias sensed my predicament. "That part is true. I also managed to spill most of the bottle on myself. I guess that is why you're so nervous. Peter told me how upset you were that he had to leave, but I promise I am more charming than he is, and infinitely more fun. You won't even notice his absence."

"I do want to thank you for taking the time out for me. I am sure you have tons of other things you could be doing." He looked at me, smiled and then bowed as if he were a knight presenting to a lady. "It would be my honor if you would please relax and enjoy yourself. The first order of business is a meal. I thought if we had the finest table at McDonald's, that would set you at ease."

Sweden has McDonald's? A juicy cheeseburger sounded perfect right about now, and away we drove.

Over two double cheeseburgers, three orders of large French fries, and good ole Coca-Cola, Mattias told me more about himself. He was successful in his career and had cabins in both Norway and Sweden. He mostly lived in Sweden and stayed in Norway only a few months of the year. He rented his Norway cabin out to tourists for most of the year as a steady source of income.

His initial success was from a series of dreamscapes he had painted, whimsical landscapes of mountains and waterfalls with fantastically colored skies. The vibrancy of colors combined with gold and silver leaf had been unparalleled in any art before his time. That had put him on the European art map. Mattias had not branched out into the American market yet with his paintings because he did not want to ride on his brother's coattails. Instead, he preferred to rely solely on his talent and word of mouth. He thrived in France and Germany doing portraits, which supplied him with most of his revenue.

Mattias was a renaissance man, a jack of all trades, that much was evident. I was amazed at how diversely talented he was. For the dozens of hobbies and interests he had, he mastered even more mediums and styles. There seemed to be nothing artistically that this man could not do. He had had a hard year of it, he said, but he didn't mention any details. I could feel a heavy weight behind his words. He had decided to take a few months off and meditate, which luckily for me coincided with my lack of a tour guide.

We fell in together, as if we had known each other from someplace far away. It was unusual for me to be so open and chatty with a stranger. Mattias was very laid back and funny, not at all like Peter, who was usually so refined. I felt instantly at ease with him. We laughed a lot during that meal, at each other's mispronunciations of words and the differences between cultures. We sat in McDonald's for hours. Around four o'clock, I glanced up and noticed there was an influx of people coming in, seemingly ordering nothing but coffee. They all seemed happy and carefree, not the usual stressed out and serious Americans I was used to at this time.

"What is going on?" I asked.

"We call it *fika,*" Mattias said. "Sweden takes coffee very seriously here, and we have several regularly scheduled coffee breaks throughout the day. It's a national requirement, and you might seriously offend someone if you say you don't have time for it. What do Americans do at this time of day?"

I laughed and said, "Rush hour."

He looked as if he didn't understand what that was, and why should he, in this beautiful coffee-laden country.

"Rush hour is typically Monday through Friday, seven to ten o'clock a.m., then three to six o'clock p.m. It can differ depending on your city, but those are good estimates. We Americans don't have time or even make time for breaks. I'm fortunate enough to have my own business now, but when I didn't, it was very stressful. We rush here and there, trying to be the first to get to the next place like it's all a contest, and we are constantly losing. We have a saying, 'If you're not first, you're last,' and that's how our society operates."

"That sounds dreadful. Does it not hurt your health?"

"Oh, it does, but there's nothing anyone can do about it except dream of the day you get to retire from your job, if you're lucky enough to have a job you can retire from. And if you do, by then you're so worn out and decrepit that you can't even enjoy all the things you've worked so hard to achieve."

"Sounds like Americans need *fika.*"

When we finished our meal, we left and wandered through the streets of Gothenburg. It was nearly dark, but tons of people were out enjoying the weather and each other's company. We walked for what felt like several miles, along the harbor at times, until I looked up and saw spotlights focused on a tall column topped with a statue of woman in a dress, watching out over the water.

"What is she doing up there?" I asked, curious.

"She is the widow of the sea. She's watching for her husband to return to her, not knowing that he has died in World War I. She is a tribute to all the sailors and all their widows. Below her are all the names of the sailors that died in the war. Do you want to walk closer and see?"

"No, I'm fine right here."

We stood there for a while in silence, and tears came to my eyes. If Mattias saw, he said nothing. Finally, we turned to go back. The air was colder now as the sun had set. The fishing boats floated like massive, seafaring skeletons against the dark, glassy water in the harbor.

"Are you tired yet?"

"A little, but I think I have a good two or three hours left in me before the jetlag will hit. Why?"

"I have one more thing I would like for us to do today if you're feeling up to it. A friend told me about it yesterday, and we won't be late, so I think you'll enjoy it before you get too tired." We stopped back into McDonald's for a caffeine boost and then were off again.

Chapter 9

I had no idea where I was or where we were going. I had complete trust in Mattias to keep me safe, but I couldn't help but think of the serial killer movies where the killer takes their victims out to a dark, secluded forest and murders them. Then again, I'd also thought Peter might be a serial killer at first. I decided I probably needed to cut true crime documentaries out of my life for a while.

We drove for what felt like forever, as the roads twisted and turned into darker shadows and all traces of civilization disappeared. We were mostly silent. The jetlag started to hit me a little harder with each tree we passed, but I am a fighter. I was determined to enjoy whatever experiences were thrown my way. I must've finally dozed off for a minute, because I don't remember the car stopping. Mattias gently woke me up, and as I looked out the window, I saw a lot of parked cars and people already milling about. Everyone was dressed in club attire, with hair colors ranging from all areas of the neon color spectrum. I did not fit in at all. I was still in my clothes from the day before, a pink floral blouse and beige pants, but I had nothing that would've matched this group anyway, so I didn't let it worry me.

Mattias opened my car door and held his hand out for me. Pitch darkness was all around us, and I could hear owls and various woodland creatures in the distance. I realized we were in the middle of the forest, and I heard music starting up from not too far away. The electricity in the air was intoxicating, the tones of people's voices buzzing around us.

"What is this place?" I asked with excitement as I felt myself start to hop to the music.

"It is an underground party for people who love to experience great music firsthand. It will go well into tomorrow morning, if there is anyone still standing. Normal clubs close much earlier, so occasionally there will be a concert with guest DJs held in some undisclosed location. You can only find out about them through word of mouth and underground news circuits. I thought you would enjoy 'letting it all out' as Americans say."

"So...it's a rave?" I asked suspiciously. I had heard about Sweden's infamous rave scene, but I wasn't a party or clubbing person. Now here I was.

"Yes, it's a rave. I wouldn't bring you to an unsafe place, Cecelia. If at any time you want to leave, we will," Mattias said, picking up on my uneasiness. "Are you hungry at all?"

"No, not yet."

I had eaten an obscene number of fries at McDonald's so I wouldn't be hungry too soon. I had learned when traveling anywhere unknown, the smartest bet was to go ahead and stock my stomach up on as much normal food as possible because I may end up in a place where I am not able to eat for hours on end.

"Okay. If you change your mind," Mattias said, pointing at a small hut that looked a lot like a vendor area at a stadium, "you have some options."

We walked towards the music, louder and more pulsating with each step. More and more people surrounded us, and more spotlights and projection lights were shining in key areas the closer we got. Mattias still had not let go of my hand, and as he led me into the crowd of people, I held on tighter. I had a pretty good sense of direction, so I felt confident that I could find the car in case I lost him, but I didn't want to take that chance in a foreign crowd in a foreign land.

We reached the front of the crowd, right beside the stage where the DJ was, and I looked around. Three giant screens as big as movie screens were set up around the stage. They were projecting multiple images, alternate forest realities to enhance our forest experience mixed with techno beats and wild, brightly colored animals running through the screens. All the images were choreographed to the music, and they changed and pulsated with each beat.

A DJ was seated at an inflatable igloo booth at the bottom of the middle screen, spinning his heart out with a variety of upbeat music. He appeared to be wearing the puffiest silver ski suit known to man and massive ski goggles on his head. Mattias was still beside me, still holding my hand. I let go of him as the rhythm washed into my bones, and we both started jumping up and down with our hands in the air. The lights would blackout every few seconds and then wash over the crowd with mixed colors and patterns. I had the biggest, cheesiest grin on my face, and it would not go away. I would occasionally glance over to make sure I was still with Mattias, and he would be right there faithfully jumping beside me like a maniac. Any trace of uneasiness I had had already disappeared. As I glanced around, we were the more normal dancers in the sea of neon and sparkle.

After several hours of dancing, the DJ said something in Swedish, which I of course could not understand. A few seconds later, all the screens transformed into dark blue forests, and the lights changed to match. A slow song began, a love song. People started turning to each other and slow dancing, and as I turned to Mattias, he took my hand and pulled me towards him. We started swaying, dancing much closer than Peter and I ever had, even in the privacy of our apartments.

I wrapped my left arm around Mattias' waist, and I rested my head on his chest. He held my right hand with his, pressed against him. He wrapped his other arm around my waist and pulled me closer. It was incredibly intimate for two people who had only known each other for one day, but I felt like we were long lost friends, reunited after decades. I closed my eyes as we swayed with the crowd. I could hear his heart racing even though we were standing in time, and it soothed me.

Dancing with him that night was different from dancing with Peter. Much different. I wasn't self-conscious at all, maybe because it was so informal, or maybe because I had had so much practice. Dancing ballroom with Peter, I still constantly stumbled over where I was going with my steps, even though we had been dancing together for months.

As the song ended, Mattias whispered in my ear, asking if I was ready to go. I was. The slow song, or dancing that close to Mattias, had slowed my energy and heart rate down tremendously from when we had been wildly jumping before, and I was suddenly exhausted. He took my hand and led me out. We early birds left the party around two a.m.

By the time we reached the car, I had done some lazy, hazy sleep brain math and realized I had been awake for nearly two days, except for that nap-mare I had had on the plane. That was the last thing I remember thinking about because as I clicked my seatbelt, my consciousness clicked off with it.

I awoke the next day, still fully clothed but in a very, very soft bed. To say it felt like a cloud doesn't give it the justice it deserves. Two solid white down comforters were on top of me, so warm and heavy I could've stayed there the rest of the week and been totally fine with it.

I sat up and looked around. The air was chilled as the comforters slid off my shoulders. The bedroom was very plain and serene looking, with dark gray walls and light gray carpet. I laughed to myself, thinking it looked like an IKEA catalog spread. My sea turtle-print suitcase sat between two open doors, against a side table with a few towels and washcloths on top. The left open door was a closet that looked as if it had a lot of men's clothes in it, and the right door I could see led to a bathroom.

Giant windows lined two of the walls, but I could only see streaks of light shining through because blackout curtains covered them. It was still enough to light up the room, and as I looked at the clock on the wall it read 4:00 p.m. Four p.m.?! If I had learned anything from yesterday, it was going to be dark in the next few hours. I had completely slept my second Sweden day away. I huffed at myself and then got over it just as quick because I knew I had been so fatigued. I smelled something delicious and decided it took priority over showering because my stomach was making a sound like a garbage can being pulled down the driveway.

I got up and opened the door. Outside were dark red wooden floors, lined with more gray walls. A banister was in the middle of the story, circling stairs leading to a lower level. On the right side of me was a closed door, and on the left was a door that I could tell led to the bathroom in my room.

Across the way on the other side of the banister was a solid gray wall, maybe the other side of the living room, lined with photographs and paintings of wildlife, including a particularly beautiful painting of a lion. The appetizing aroma seemed to be coming from my left, towards the light, and I looked over to see a more open floor plan on that side.

I walked to the end of the hall, where I was greeted by Mattias in a long-sleeved white shirt and jeans, cooking fish in an immaculate white and stainless-steel kitchen. To the right of the kitchen was a simple farm table with basic chairs. Full panel windows lined the corner for about ten feet either way.

Around the corner, on the other side of that gray wall, was the living room, with a large white and gray-patterned rug with a large gray leather sofa against the wall and a fifty-inch flat-screen TV on the opposite side. Just past the couch was the front door.

"Please make yourself at home. What is mine is yours."

I turned to face Mattias, who was hard at work on his fish.

"How did I get in here? I don't remember anything."

"I carried you. You were pretty passed out, so I placed you in my bed because it's the more comfortable of the two. I took the guest bedroom. I decided to let you sleep off your jetlag and then continue with plans tomorrow, if that is all right. I took the liberty while you slept to go into town to the *Feskekörka* and buy some salmon and crab for you. Do you like seafood?"

"Yes, I love most everything except oysters. What was the word you said? *Fishfork?* What is that?"

He laughed and said, "*Feskekörka*, I think it translates to Fish Church. It is a local fish market here in Gothenburg that carries all the fresh catches of the day. Restaurants are in there, but you can also purchase whatever you would like to bring home and cook for yourself."

"It smells divine. Is there anything I can help you with?"

He pointed me to the plates and silverware, and I set up the table and poured two glasses of water.

"I love your home, the way you've decorated, or lack thereof. It's so simplistic yet comfortable," I said.

"Thank you, I have found that having a plain surface to view inspires the mind to fill it with visions. The more simplistic I can create my surroundings to be, the more my mind overreacts to inspire my next work."

"That is so true. I get it. It's good to be bored because then your mind creates something to fill the gaps. Non-creative minds see serenity, but creative minds see chaos in the stillness."

He looked at me for a solid minute, his deep blue eyes flickering with light as if he were absorbing some prophecy I had just foretold. His face and expression changed after a few moments, softened in some way that I couldn't describe from visual cues but felt deep into my soul. My cheeks blushed and I glanced down at the floor. I felt he had just seen me completely exposed.

He continued to watch me for a moment longer, but I did not feel uncomfortable or even a little bit awkward. I rather liked him blatantly staring at me. In my mind, I felt as if he had some superpower, which he was using on me.

Peter never looked at me, understood me, like that. I looked up at Mattias, and our gaze met for a few more moments until I said, "I think your sauce is burning."

He snapped out of his transfixion and wheeled around to stir the garlic butter cream sauce he had made for the crab. I giggled silently to myself and finished setting the table.

Mattias delivered two beautifully colored plates to the table. He had cooked for me salmon with a dill sauce, crab with a garlic butter cream sauce, and fingerling potatoes with butter and tiny bright red berries that tasted like raspberries on top.

"What are these berries?"

"Those are lingonberries. A lot of Scandinavian dishes feature them. They are traditional and go with pretty much every dish. A lot of times I like to use them with pork, but I thought tonight I would mix it up a bit for you."

"It's all delicious, better than any restaurant could've made, I'm positive. I can't even cook this good, and I like to think I could star on the Food Network. Peter didn't tell me that you cook. Or much about you at all."

"Peter also didn't mention how captivatingly beautiful you are."
I felt myself blush a deep red. Mattias was his brother's brother all
right, good at randomly throwing me off my game.

"I am sorry," he continued. "I didn't mean to make you
uncomfortable. I know that you're my brother's girlfriend. I only
meant to say that I feel a raw connection with you that I have not
felt in a long time. I have never been able to describe to someone
my visions and have them recite their understanding back to me
so accurately, as if we're on the same frequency. Is that cliché?
That is cliché. I'll say no more about it."

I laughed at him answering his own question. "Thank you for
saying that. I appreciate it. I do agree and I do understand what
you mean. I wasn't expecting it is all."

Later after we had cleaned up from dinner, we sat on the
leather sofa and watched Swedish crime shows. *Watched* is too
loose a term— Mattias watched and I stared blankly. Swedish
shows don't have subtitles when the audience watching is also
Swedish. I made it through almost two episodes before I gave up
and decided to take a much-needed shower and go to bed early.

"Thank you again for the delicious dinner, Mattias. Good
night!"

"*God natt!* Rest well. In the morning, we head north!"

Chapter 10

I sat up from underneath the down comforters and looked at the clock, which showed 1:00 a.m. My internal clock was horribly backwards, and I was wide awake. I was used to starting my days back in New York early, but not this early. I didn't know what the Swedish custom was, either, but probably not 1:00 a.m.

I walked into the bathroom and gasped at what I saw in the mirror. My curly mane of blonde hair was standing up on end in a frazzled mess, and I remembered I had been so tired last night after I took a shower that I had gone to sleep with my hair wet. Curly Hair Cardinal Rule #1: ALWAYS fully dry before bed if you want to look decent in the morning. Luckily, I had the foresight to pack my trusty curling iron, so I ran some water on my hands and dampened the trouble spots. I usually made a rule to avoid curling my hair when it was wet. It can lead to dryness, plus I invariably cringed at the sizzling sound it makes, as if it's frying in a vat. Desperate times called for desperate measures, so here goes.

Pleased with the soft curls that now framed my face, I spritzed on some travel-sized hairspray I had stashed in my suitcase in case of emergency. Mattias had said we were heading north, so I chose a pastel pink sweater and slightly larger than normal jeans so I could put leggings on underneath them. I had been a little chilly walking around in Gothenburg, so surely two layers would do the trick. I doubled my socks also. Satisfied with my layering skills, I walked out into the hallway.

Mattias was already in the kitchen, wearing a light green cable knitted turtleneck sweater that accented his deep blue eyes.

"You're up already?"

"*God morgon!* I don't sleep much. I heard you moving around, so I decided to get ready too. We have quite a drive ahead of us."

He was cooking again, frying eggs, bacon, and something that looked like a black sausage.

"I included a local delight for you to try."

He handed me a picturesque plate of eggs, bacon, and the unidentified thing with lingonberries on top.

"What is this?" It smelled odd, not bad, but not like something I would keep in my kitchen either.

"Blood pudding. Similar to American sausage, I think. It's an acquired taste but very traditional."

It was salty, and I didn't like it. I scrunched my nose and ate the lingonberries off the top. Mattias laughed, ate his whole portion in one fell swoop, then asked for mine that I wouldn't eat.

"Where are we headed?" I asked. "You said north, how far?"

"Quite far, almost to the top of the world."

I didn't understand at first. I forgot we were so far up already that we were almost in traveling distance of the North Pole.

I sat up straighter in my chair. "I put on two layers of pants and socks just in case," I said, patting my legs. I loved to be prepared.

"A good start, to be sure. You Americans are so funny with your layers and determination, but that's okay. I have extra coats and blankets I will be taking with us if we need them. Of course, we may not need anything extra, and you may be overdressed. It depends on if the weather is feeling mischievous or not."

The first few hours of the car ride consisted of listening to metal music, none of which I was familiar with, but Mattias seemed very into it. Some of it I might've heard at the rave several nights ago, but I wasn't sure. Either way, it wasn't really my style. About five hours in, my ears hurting by now, we stopped at a McDonald's to grab a quick bite and stretch our legs. I had no clue that McDonald's restaurants were so abundant in Sweden, but I welcomed the familiarity. Another five hours of metal music and another snack and stretch break later, I asked Mattias how much further we lacked.

"About ten more hours now."

"We're taking a forty-hour round-trip road trip?" I asked with a French fry hanging out of my mouth.

Mattias looked amused. "Yes, we are going to Abisko National Park. I think you'll appreciate it. There are several things to do there, and you will get a good experience of Sweden in the summertime. I have not been in some years either, so it'll be like brand new for both of us. You are welcome to try and get some sleep in the car. I have had quite a bit of coffee, so I will be fully awake. I will change the music since you seem not to be enjoying my metal taste."

"No, I can stay awake. But I'm going to get a McFlurry." Bad idea. Five ABBA songs back into the road trip, my blood sugar skyrocketed, and I passed out midway through "Dancing Queen." I woke up four hours later to hear Mattias quietly humming to himself. When I looked out the window, the landscape had started to change to more back roads and mountains than cityscapes and civilization. I sat up in my seat.

Mattias looked over at me and said, "Welcome back! We are going to stop at another McDonald's for one last stretch break as we come across it, and then it will not be much farther."

I smiled. "Is McDonald's your favorite restaurant?"

"No, but it might be easier for you to have something that you are used to, so I don't over-Sweden you with too much culture."

"Culture can be a good thing. If more people would bother to get more familiar with different cultures, I think the world would be a better place. What was that music you were humming? It didn't sound metal."

"Swedish folk songs. I feel that they should be sung when going through the mountains. Would you like me to sing you some and culture you?"

"Yes, please."

He started with "The Sound of Music."

I interrupted him. "That's not Swedish!"

He laughed a cute and whimsical laugh. "I was just making sure you were awake enough to appreciate the live concert you are about to behold."

Mattias then sang about ten or twelve folk songs, most of them in his native Swedish tongue. I didn't know the songs, except for a couple of them like "Sankta Lucia" that I had heard before.

"What are some of your American songs?" I thought for a minute, trying to figure out what the most patriotic songs were that I knew all the words to, and then began singing the most patriotic, American songs I could think of, complete with jazz hands and dashboard drums when appropriate. Imagine being at a USO tour in the 1950s, and that was my concert.

My big patriotic finale was the "National Anthem." I was shocked when I was able to hit the high note without my voice cracking. I cleared my throat. "And now for selections from the South." I sang two of my all-time favorite songs, one from the 1960s and one from the early 1970s. Charlie always said when it came to music, I should've been a flower child. My rendition was slow and deep, my voice wailing at the high notes in a mournful fashion. I missed a few notes, but it was decent.

"These songs both mention New Orleans, why?" Mattias asked.

"The South is a very inspiring place in general. Lots of soul and spirituality are abundantly clear in the people and the art that comes from there, whether it be music, movies, books, or even food. Have you heard of country music before? That's about as American as you can get. In certain areas of the South people tend to get downright real offended if you don't know things we consider to be common knowledge, such as who Johnny Cash is." I laughed, hearing my Southern drawl come out when saying "downright real offended."

"I think I have heard of Cash, but I am not familiar with his songs."

I put on my deepest, manliest voice and began rendition of a few of his songs in the slowest and most mournful voice I could muster. When I had finished, we rode in quiet for a few moments. I started singing a country song about a soldier in Vietnam in a soft and low voice. The artist's ability to capture Americana in the times of Vietnam had made this one of my favorite songs, and now it seemed like a fitting song to finish off my American karaoke playlist. By the time I got to the last line, the tears were flowing freely from my eyes.

"That is beautiful. A folk song?"

"No, that's another country song. It gets down into the nitty-gritty of your soul and exposes all the ugly parts, but the magic of it is that the songs are about experiences that everyone universally shares, no matter who you are. Being jealous, drinking yourself to death, your favorite dog, your worst ex, or the most haunting moment of your life is probably a country song. That's why country music resonates with so many people."

"Vietnam was a long time ago, yes?"

"Yes, but don't you feel like you were there yesterday after hearing that song?"

"Yes, I felt the pain of loss. Do you know another one that lingers like that?"

I did. I started singing another country song. Mattias was the one who teared up this time.

We rode in silence while my vocal cords rested.

"Do you want to hear one of my favorite songs ever? In English it translates to 'None Shall Sleep.'" I began singing "Nessun Dorma" in Italian the best that I could. I'd never attempted to sing it for anyone, but somehow I felt like Mattias would appreciate it no matter how well I could pull it off.

"That is such a beautiful song. How do you know an Italian song?"

"I'm a bit of an opera nerd. Pavarotti made it famous, but I saw Aretha Franklin singing it on an awards show when I was little. Ever since then, I've been obsessed with it. I've been trying to learn Italian, but I don't know if I'm pronouncing the words correctly enough to do them justice. It's a much more effective song when you hear it sung by a professional."

"It is an opera song? What opera?"

"*Turandot*, about a princess looking for a suitor."

"Have you ever seen this *Turandot*? There are operas in New York, has Peter ever taken you?"

"No, actually he hasn't. I don't think it's ever even come up in conversation that I would like to go." In fact, Mattias putting it so simply made me think about all the dates we had had. I couldn't remember him ever asking if there was anything I would like to do.

We just did what he was already going to do.

Our last McDonald's stop was in Lulea, roughly five hours from Abisko, according to Mattias, and a full seventeen hours since we had left the previous morning. The time was now 7:00 p.m., and I realized the sun hadn't fully set. Had I just not noticed it? Maybe I had been so lost in my vocal arrangements that I didn't even pay attention. I wondered if it sets later the farther north you are.

No matter, I was just along for the ride at this point. I usually hated road trips, but this one had been fun and relaxing, and majestic, and I was enjoying Mattias' company immensely. I suddenly realized I hadn't called Peter to check on him. He hadn't called me either, so I decided not to bother him while he was working.

I stocked up on French fries again, and an extra-large Coca-Cola so that I could pack away the caffeine for when I needed it. I didn't get a McFlurry this time since one sugar crash today was enough. Mattias must've been feeling the drive, because he scarfed down two burgers this time, and at least two extra-large soda refills by the time we had left. We refilled our sodas once more and headed back out on the road. The scenery changed to mountains, snow, and wilderness; and I could see waterfalls in the distance.

Mattias glanced over at me. "We will almost make it but not quite, but you'll still get to see the full effect."

"What are we trying to get to?"

"The top of the mountain, to see the Midnight Sun. The way the earth is positioned, the sun does not set at Abisko during several of the summer months. During the winter months, you can see the Northern Lights from the park. It's a great attraction for tourists and locals alike. Most people come by train, which is not much shorter, but it is much easier to travel. I thought since you had all week, it would be fun to make it a road trip so that you could experience Sweden in all its glory." I was getting giddy just listening to him talk about it.

"There is a hiking trail that goes up to the top of the mountain. I think you are probably a fast walker, so I estimate we'll be at the top about one o'clock a.m. Not quite midnight, but it'll be fine. There are benches when we get to the top to look out over the valley and sunset."

"Oh wow, that's amazing! I had no idea how far north I was. I'm so excited now! I love experiencing natural wonders."

Conveniently, as always, my camera was just an arm's length away in the backseat if I could remember to use it and not get caught up in my surroundings. So far, I had not taken any photos, which was quite a tragedy for me. I had been so wrapped up in my travel arrangements, photography hadn't even crossed my mind. I still had a few days, though, so I was going to make the most of it.

Chapter 11

We arrived at Abisko and started hiking up the trail. It was around eighty degrees outside, not great weather for layers. Mattias had dried fruits and water in his backpack, plus two rolled blankets just in case we needed them. I opted to carry only my camera and leave my coat behind. I was glad I had worn my boots. They weren't quite hiking boots, but they were as close as I had.

Going up the mountain was beautiful in and of itself. Most of it was heavily wooded areas. Moss covered streams ran beside us or under us for most of the way, with adorable rustic footbridges scattered throughout the trail. I saw lots more of the twin flowers Peter had pointed out to me at his parents' house. They seemed to be abundant in their natural habitat, and I instantly knew why his dad had tried so hard to make them feel at home in Gothenburg. They were wild and fairy-like, and being mixed in with various other wildflowers throughout the trail gave it a magical, surreal feeling. We hiked for about an hour and a half, stopping for me to take pictures along the way, until we found a secluded spot that seemed to be away from the rest of civilization.

This spot was beautifully perfect, a nice little clearing just off the trail where we could see down over the full landscape of the mountain we were on. Mountains, valleys, streams, and waterfalls galore lay before us as far as the eye could see. If I weren't there in person, I would've assumed it was a movie set. It reminded me of the paintings of America before it was settled, when it was wild and free.

Even though it was warm, we were on the windward side, so the wind was still a bit catchy. We spotted a well-worn bench on the side of the path. Mattias unrolled the blankets, draped one over the seat, and then wrapped the other one around our shoulders for comfort. The sun did not fully set while we waited. The darkest the sky got was like early evening in Savannah, just a few heavy shadows gone as quickly as they appeared. We sat there for a while in silence, marveling in the picturesque landscape until Mattias started quoting a beautiful poem, which seemed to oddly be in tune with our surroundings.

"That's beautiful! Did you write it?"

"No, that was my dear friend, Lord Byron, a poem called 'So We'll Go No More A Roving.'"

"So, you just happen to randomly recite Scottish poetry too, amongst your many other talents?"

"When the mood strikes me. I spent a summer there studying the landscape, and I picked up several extra of the local charms," he said, pausing for a minute, lost in his thoughts.

"I have traveled through a large part of Europe over the years, searching for new inspirations for my artwork. There is nothing quite like experiencing different cultures to open your creative processes."

"Aren't you just an enigma." I said and as he smiled, I noticed how his eyes crinkled in the corners. I took a few pictures of the two of us sitting on the bench, and then a few of him either smiling at me or looking off into the wild. He paused for a few minutes, then asked very thoughtfully but hesitantly, "May I ask you something? Why were you crying at the Sailor's Widow statue? I haven't seen anyone react that way."

I didn't think he'd seen me, I was in stealth mode. I started to answer, just as a seagull with a heart-shaped scratch and no right foot landed a few feet away, unafraid to be close to us. I smiled, waved at it and snapped a picture. Mattias noticed but did not say anything.

"Did Peter not tell you? I'm a widow."

"Oh, I'm sorry. No, he didn't tell me. We don't talk as much as we used to. What happened, if I may ask?"

I smiled and started telling him my story. "I saw the most beautiful man when I was fifteen. He was glowing the first time I saw him. Not really glowing, I'm not psychotic, but I knew there was something else there. Something no one could see unless they knew where to look. I still remember like it was yesterday. He was wearing jeans and a maroon T-shirt underneath a denim jacket. The voice of God was telling me I had to get to know him. I was so nervous to talk to him so I did the only thing I could think to do. I wrote him a letter, asking if we could be friends. I'd made a complete idiot out of myself, but I knew I needed to at least try. He called me a few nights later, and a month after that, he baptized me. From then on, we were pretty much inseparable. We got married fresh out of high school, and he died when he was twenty-seven. It was almost three years ago now."

"That was a courageous move, putting yourself out there by writing a letter to a stranger," Mattias said.

"It was pretty gutsy, but it did work. We started going to Bible studies a week later. A month later, he baptized me himself, and then we were nearly inseparable until he died," I was almost surprised at myself for not crying while telling Mattias the details of our story.

"I am deeply sorry for your loss. May I ask how someone so young died?"

"I asked myself that for years. He had a brain aneurysm. One minute he was there and the next minute he was gone, no symptoms and no warning. I thought my life was ending. Everything crashed down on top of me, and I couldn't breathe. I couldn't think, I couldn't sleep or eat. He was the best thing that had ever happened to me. The only life I had ever known or wanted to know was with him. Suddenly I was completely alone. I was so angry for a long time, with God for taking him, with myself for not doing more, being more. I blamed myself for all of it, did I not love him enough? Did I not appreciate him enough? Had I not prayed over him enough? Was I not thankful enough? Was I not a good enough Christian, or person, or wife? Was there something I had done to deserve this kind of punishment? I knew it wasn't my fault, but I couldn't wrap my head around anything. I was furious and heartbroken at the same time. Each passing day made me dizzy with grief. About a year ago, my best friend suggested I move away, to start the life that my husband and I had been planning for ourselves. So, I picked up the pieces of my life that I had left, and I moved to New York to start fresh. A few months later I met Peter, and now I'm sitting here in Sweden."

"You knew your husband was for you when you saw him for the first time? How did you know such a thing? What did you mean when you said he was glowing?"

"Yes, I knew. The voice of God just spoke to me, and I knew that was that. When my dad first saw my mom, he said she was glowing. She was his nurse, and soon as he got out of the hospital he proposed to her. They've been madly in love ever since. I think spirits are attracted to similar spirits. So, when your spirit is right, you radiate goodness and someone with a like spirit will recognize it. I think that's what 'love at first sight' is. I don't know, maybe not. My parents have been married for forty years, so it could be true."

"You heard an actual voice?"

"No, not for me. It's like a feeling in my heart. It's hard to explain, but it's kind of like intuition. When someone says, 'follow your heart,' I have found for me that means when God is speaking to me. If I listen, I won't be mistaken or mislead. If I go against it and do what I think is best, then I find out pretty quickly I've messed up and have to go back."

"What does being a Christian mean? You are saying you believe in something you cannot see, and you live your life based on feelings?"

I smiled a wide smile and said, "No, quite the contrary. You can see God all around you. You just have to pay attention." He looked confused.

"You don't have to believe me. You can ask Him yourself." I pointed to my little buddy.

Now he looked even more bewildered. "What are you talking about?"

"That seagull right there, I've known him since high school. His name is Major Birdie Biddle. For cheap dates, Charlie and I used to go feed seagulls. One bird would always show up, missing his right foot and had a heart-shaped scratch on his beak. I felt bad for him, so I would give him his own piece of bread. After Charlie died, I started going to the cemetery and taking photos to help me process my grief. That seagull was there each week. Then, when I moved to New York, he would show up on my balcony every few weeks, same missing foot, same scratch."

"That is not possible. There is no way that same seagull followed you around the world and that it is God in disguise. How do you know there are not multiple seagulls that look similar? Or that it is a coincidence?"

I pulled out my phone and showed him a screenshot of the seagull's picture hanging in my gallery. "You're right. Maybe it's not. Maybe it is. Maybe it's my husband sending me a sign, telling me things are going to turn out all right, telling me that he's in Heaven. You say it's impossible, yet here we sit, not even ten feet away from a bird that looks identical to the one in this picture. You can ask Peter. He's seen him on my balcony." Mattias looked genuinely confused.

"God is wherever you look, if you're looking. The earth is full of stories like this: a dog or cat starts appearing at a certain time; a butterfly or a dragonfly appears at just the right moment after a loved one passes; a flower that has never bloomed suddenly blooms on the birthday of a someone who's passed on; a tree that was dead for years mysteriously starts growing after someone passes; a song that rarely plays on the radio comes on; you smell their perfume or cologne when no one is around, and so on. The accounts are limitless. Small miracles happen all the time, but if you're not paying attention, you'll miss what's all around you.

God wants us to know that He's present, even in our darkest hours, so He sends little signals to remind us to keep going and trust Him."

We sat there in silence for quite a while. I braced for impact, preparing myself for what was coming my way. I was expecting an argument or a strong disagreement, something I was pretty used to as a Christian. Anytime I mentioned God around a non-believer, that person would usually roll their eyes, which was often followed by an argument and subsequent mockery of my faith. But none of that happened now.

The sounds of the mountain were all around us as we watched the gorgeous landscape below. After about thirty minutes, I was still waiting for a response of any sort, but nothing came. I looked over to see how Mattias was doing. He was still looking off into the non-sunset, apparently contemplating all I had said as if he were trying to understand and not mock me.

Mattias spoke finally. "You packed up and moved to a foreign land just like that? Were you terrified?"

"Well, yes. But what choice did I have? Getting through each day was so hard for me for a long time. It seemed like the only thing I could do was to start over, and now I'm living in an entirely new adventure. It was challenging at first, but I don't regret it. I needed a fresh start to move on, to keep living." I decided to change the subject. "Why are you and Peter not close? He hasn't mentioned any reason to me."

"No, and he probably never will. He keeps most things to himself. He's always been that way. We are close as brothers, but we are not close as friends. We grew apart in our lives. Peter is the oldest, and he feels a responsibility to look out for me and our little brother, Caspar. Sometimes this comes across as pushing us around, and that doesn't sit well with us.

"Peter said I should have followed him and our parents and been more studious, but I chose the more artsy, bohemian life. I'm ashamed to admit that I had to rely on him financially after the first few years of school, which put another divide between us. I have since paid him back, but I know he still feels as if he was the one in the right. He doesn't agree with my life choices in general. He doesn't believe in making mistakes but believes in planning out life ten steps ahead. He is stubborn and responsible, and he thinks I'm immature and childish. He's frequently stated that I should take things more seriously. He's not wrong; I was usually too unpredictable for him. Make no mistake though, he can go so far off routine that you wouldn't even recognize him."

I thought about our first dinner together, how he had shown up and appeared as a completely different person from the serious curator I had first met. I suddenly felt that maybe I didn't know Peter quite as well. Maybe what I knew was the narrative in my head, and not the actual man. We watched the landscape for a bit longer in more silence. Finally, Mattias spoke again. I did not recognize the poem he was reciting, but the words gave me a feeling of hopelessness for the lovers portrayed in it.

"That is beautiful too, but morose."

"It is called 'The Shadows' by Iain Crichton Smith." He took a deep, slow breath, and I felt he was about to say something intensely deep. "Peter is there for the people he loves. He is a good man. Unapologetically loyal."

He hesitated before he spoke again. "Some months ago, I was at the very lowest point of my life. I had locked myself away in my house and turned off my phone. I took too many pills and drank too much alcohol. My saving moment was that I was supposed to have dinner with my parents, and I had completely forgotten. When they had not heard from me the day of and the day after, they broke the door down and found me nearly lifeless, but alive. My heart was barely beating.

"They pumped my stomach and put me on fluids for a week. I was so dehydrated and worn down. I am not a drug addict. Alcoholic maybe, but drugs, no. I had never, ever done anything like that before. I had not planned to in the first place, but I just needed to escape. Peter flew over immediately and sat with me in the hospital every day. He didn't leave my side."

I now faintly remembered Peter saying he couldn't make my RSVP showing because he had to take care of family business. This must've been that.

"Peter was so mad about it. He still hasn't forgiven me. To him, that just backs up his feeling that he must always look out for me and that I'm irresponsible. I am doing better now. I still have hard days. I haven't felt inspired enough to do much painting lately, so I have given myself off a few months. The only artistic thing I have done is compose music. Peter wanted me to show you around because he felt it would be a good chance for me to get out and get motivated. He was not wrong." He smiled sweetly.

"I'm so sorry, for all of it, truly I am. I am enjoying spending so much time with you too. For me, you've been like a breath of fresh air. May I ask what happened?"

He paused. His eyes fixated on something, somewhere, a million miles away.

"My girlfriend had dumped me several months before. We met at one of my art exhibitions in Gothenburg. She was one of the waitresses serving hors d'oeuvres, and we just hit it off instantly. She was Scottish, hip, cool, free-spirited, and exciting. Everything I thought I wanted. Her parents had died when she was young, so she had grown up in multiple households with people constantly rotating in and out of her life. She was constantly surrounded by people, both good and bad." He lowered his head, thinking about the painful memories.

"I thought I would be the one to change her reality, to show her that there were people in the world she could count on. We didn't talk about marriage or the future, we just went from moment to moment. I should have asked her; we should have talked about it, but it just didn't come up. We were wild and passionate, enjoying life in the here and now. I was madly in love with her. I followed her everywhere. That's how I ended up in Scotland for a summer, taking in the poetry and local culture." Mattias paused, sighing heavily before he continued.

"We were together for three years. You think you know a person by then. She started to change in the end. The last few months we fought a lot more, about stupid, trivial things. I had no clue as to why, or maybe I wasn't paying enough attention. One day during *fika,* she did something that took me by surprise. She sat her coffee down and looked me square in the eyes with no emotion whatsoever. I did not recognize her. She said she could not be with me, that I was bringing her down. I begged and pleaded with her for answers, for her to change her mind. I had no idea where any of this was coming from because she hadn't talked to me about it before. She said she didn't want to be tied down to anyone. Finally, she told me she'd had an abortion several months earlier. I was blindsided." I gasped as a tear rolled down his face.

"I felt as if a weight had been dropped in my stomach. She did not want to be a mother. She'd never wanted to be a mother or a wife. She didn't want the childhood she had experienced to be burdened upon someone else. She could not and did not want to take care of a child or be tied down to any man for the rest of her life. Being pregnant had made her realize this even more." I could easily sympathize with his pain and loss.

"I've always wanted a son. I don't know if that's what our baby was, but that's what I imagine. I would have wanted him, if given a choice. I would have raised him on my own. I would have done anything. I happily would have kept him and been a single dad, but she did not give me the option. She made all these decisions without me and moved to Spain to start a new and more exciting life almost overnight, fresh without consequences. My work suffered tremendously after that. I couldn't paint. I couldn't do anything. I locked myself away in my cabin, with minimal contact with the outside world other than my parents occasionally. Soon in the quiet and solitude, I began to hear music in my head, and I wrote it into reality."

I did the only thing I could think to do—I wrapped my arms around him as he sat beside me on the bench. I whispered to him, "I am so sorry for everything. No one should ever have to go through that." He held onto me tightly, sobbing quietly after a few deep breaths. I imagined myself absorbing his pain so that he could begin to heal. I kissed the side of his head and held him there for a long time, blankets wrapped around us, nothing but cool mountain air and serenity surrounding us.

As I held him gently in my arms, I realized the man I had spent the last few days with was just a shell, a façade of the man before me now. Not so long ago, I was in his shoes. It took immense courage for Mattias to become the man of the last few days, to go on as if nothing were wrong when he was still so broken and raw inside. In that moment, I loved and appreciated him for it.

Mattias continued opening up to me. "I felt like such a failure, like I had let her down, let myself down, and most importantly, let down our baby. I haven't told anyone the whole story, not even Peter. My mother knew something terrible had happened. She could sense it in me, but I couldn't even bear to tell her the whole truth. It is strange that I felt so comfortable with you as soon as I saw you listening to the music. No one else knew about it. I do not understand how you could have known how much it meant to me."

I let go of him, and we both returned to normal sitting positions.

"Mattias, why didn't you tell anyone? That's such a heavy load to carry alone."

"I was so ashamed. I had no control over costing my baby his life. I spoke to no one. What would I have said? I felt so hopeless, like I was drowning." Mattias sighed.

How could she break this gentle man in such an awful way? "She should have taken your feelings into account and considered you. It was rude and cruel of her to do anything else. She knew what a kind heart you have."

Mattias nodded ever so slightly.

"I can't imagine anyone letting you go," I said before I realized what I was saying. "I'm sorry, I shouldn't have said that." He looked at me gently but said nothing. For a fleeting second, I saw his face lighten. We sat in silence for a long while.

After about twenty minutes, I spoke. "I don't think it was your fault at all. There is a darkness in all of us. In her, in you, in me. It's what we do with it and how we choose to affect the people around us that makes the difference. Don't ever be afraid to speak your truth to anyone. You'll never overcome your darkness if you don't. And you certainly can't begin to heal."

He sat up a little straighter, a little more determined than the man he had been a few minutes ago, as if he wanted to move on from this moment. "Are you and my brother serious as a couple?" he asked when he spoke again. That was a change of subject if I ever heard one.

I sighed and shook my head slightly. "I don't know. We don't talk about the future. We just kind of exist in the moment."

"We have that in common, I suppose."

"I have to trust in God that he knows what's going on with my life and where I'm going."

"I don't much believe in your God. If He were real and is nothing but love and goodness as you say, then there wouldn't be suffering in the world. Why would God allow so much senseless pain and death?"

"He believes in you, or we wouldn't be having this conversation. The feeling of love is cheapened in today's world because most of the time it's not love that we feel. We get caught up in the next big thing, the next big emotion. When it fades as quickly as it came, we assume love must not be real, or that love is not something we can maintain. When it is real, love is rare and glorious. God's love is beautiful and powerful like that. He works through us all the time. Death is not a bad thing. It's a hard thing to deal with, especially when it happens too soon, but it is a part of the cycle. There is a season for everything. I can't begin to explain to you why it all happens, only that it does happen for a reason. A higher plan is at play that we can't possibly understand because we're only human. That's where faith in God comes in the equation. I trust Him because I can't see the big picture."

"That is a way for saying you don't know, and you just leave it all up to chance."

"I don't know, no one does, but it's not chance. When Charlie died, his organs were donated to the local hospital. He was in perfect health, and nothing was wrong with him at all. We talked about organ donation a lot. It was something we felt very strongly about. If something tragic ever happened to us, we wanted to pay it forward and try and help someone else. I have to believe that he died so that others could live, that his death wasn't wasted. They say if you receive an organ from someone, you take on a few of their mannerisms. I don't know if that's true, but it's a nice thing to think about. Your physical presence is able to live through someone while your spirit lives in Heaven? It comforts me sometimes, thinking I might pass Charlie's heart on the street. God is in the details."

"I thought the devil was in the details?"

"A common misconception. Originally, it was God in the details. God is the origin. God is the detail. If you think you can see the big picture without God, then you aren't looking close enough at the details. And if you're only looking at the details instead of the big picture, then you're missing God completely. It's all intertwined. As far as most problems in the world go, mankind creates its problems through greed, ignorance, and corruption. We didn't start out that way. We didn't start out with banks and governments and money and political rivalries. God gave us the power to make our own decisions or fall. See, God's plan and free will go hand in hand if you think about it."

Mattias seemed to be mulling over what I was saying.

"God has a plan for you, which you have free will to accept or not. Everyone is responsible for his or her own choices, but instead of owning up to them, they blame God when things go wrong and fail to thank God when things go right. No one wants to hear the truth because it scares them. If you hear the truth, then you have to do something about it, and people would rather pretend to be ignorant than be held accountable. There's no escaping that we will all be held accountable one day. People don't want to feel as if they're mortal, because if they do, then they won't feel in control. No one is in control. Not really. It's a false sense of security. So, people blame God, saying that He isn't real and that people should only find joy in earthly delights." I could feel myself starting to get animated.

Mattias took a deep, contemplating breath as I continued. "Rates of suicide around the world are growing higher and higher as we're led to believe that life doesn't matter, only instant gratification and pursuing the next big thing. When that fails, people can't admit to themselves that their situation is less than ideal because of the decisions they made themselves, so they ignore the truth. An old hymn talks about how we pass through this world, that it's not home to us. You have to remember to rise above the world. It is hard—at times it feels impossible, but when your heart is tired and you don't recognize the world around you, it's because it's not your world to begin with. Not if your sights are set on heaven."

"I see no evidence of God, though, or Heaven. No definitive evidence exists that says He created the world," Mattias said.

I was careful to be steady and calm in the tone of my response. "Okay, consider this. Free your mind. Open it and think about one question: *What if?* Your mind is telling you to doubt because you've been more exposed to more doubt than faith. I could give you all the go-to arguments for Christianity, but even I think they're old and worn out. One of them describes cutting up a watch and putting it in a glass."

"That sounds unnecessary. What purpose does that serve?"

"The idea is that if you can't throw a bunch of watch pieces together in a glass and it comes out whole, then how can you say something so complicated as the universe can just happen with a bang."

"That seems illogical. Of course, watches were made by men, and they have to be pieced together by hand."

"And of course, that's the Christian argument behind it. If you can't bang pieces of a watch together and create a brand new one, how in the universe did a universe happen out of particles? It seems silly that that's even an argument that we have to have, but that's the world we live in."

"Fair point. Continue."

"Let your mind wander with me for a moment in the actual reality of the world, okay? Don't immediately think, 'No, that's not possible,' just think 'What if?' How many major cities have you visited in Sweden? How many are there outside of Sweden? How many major cities are in the whole world, and how many of those have you been to?"

"Countless numbers, but you could try to count them if you researched every possible area."

"Just stay with me. Now, how many small towns, neighborhoods, and areas outside of those cities do you think there are, and how many of those have you visited? An infinite number, right? Now, how many trees, any variety, are in each one? Each suburb, city, county, country, how many?"

"That is impossible to tell. Where are you going with this? Are you saying it is possible to count every single tree in the world?"

"No, what I'm saying is that trees are physical. Something you can feel, see, and experience."

"And?"

"And they're on your very own planet, but you don't have a clue as to how to accurately answer my question. After you count the trees, physically counting them all one by one, then you go to grains of sand on beaches and count them one by one. They're big enough to count, so count them. Every beach, every grain. Then when you've finished with all the trees and all the beaches, you go to the sandstone and the deserts and count those grains as well."

"Now that is impossible. That would be madness. You would have to estimate how many there were."

"Yes, you would, if you wanted to get through it in your lifetime. You would have no actual physical proof of my questions unless you used a mathematical formula to calculate it out. Even still, I would say you were being lazy because the evidence is right in front of you, and you didn't even bother to take the time to find out. That's madness."

"What you are asking is impossible to do. Even if you had a group of people doing it, there are no guarantees that it would be 100 percent accurate."

"Exactly. That is my exact point. You can see, feel, and experience all those things directly in front of you, and you still don't, can't, know all there is to know. Non-believers tend to argue that God is not scientific, and not enough scientific evidence is provided for Him. But no one even knows all there is to know about our planet. We still haven't explored all the oceans and seas on earth yet. We don't even know how many trees are on our planet. Isn't it arrogant and pompous for someone to say that God doesn't exist just because they can't see Him? You can't possibly see all the trees on your planet, but that doesn't mean they don't exist. How stupid people are to think that our awareness is bigger than the universe just because we believe it so."

Mattias laughed. "Peter did say you were a character builder, that you are unwavering in your opinions on the world."

"Well, that's true when I'm passionate about something. Jesus says in John 10 that He has sheep in many pastures and that He must bring them all together. Sometimes it's taken out of context for arguments to demonstrate that there is so much that we don't know. Who are the other sheep? We may not be the only sheep, figuratively speaking, and we can't even find out. We don't know if there's another earth in another solar system somewhere out in the wide vast universe. We can't find the edge of the universe! We can't even be sure how our universe came to be! Scientists are constantly changing their theories based on new evidence. Shouldn't that be evidence enough that you don't have all the answers?" I noticed Mattias grinning at me, but I was on a roll now and I kept on.

"How can humans say that God doesn't exist when humans themselves are nothing in comparison to time and space as a whole? Humans are just a speck of being in the infinite, and we think we have the authority to say that God isn't real? We just make him laugh!"

"And furthermore!" His eyebrows were arched in a highly amused expression as I continued my speech. I was getting overly passionate now, not heated but animated, and my voice was getting squeaky. He seemed to be entertained, so I continued. "More scientifically, mathematics!"

He laughed. "What about mathematics?"

"Mathematics originated ages ago, but how were the scholars who created it so intelligent and enlightened, and so above themselves enough to be able to recognize mathematical certainties found in nature? Have you ever heard of the Golden Ratio?"

"No, I have not."

"It is a number that equals 1.618, and it is present everywhere in our world, from art to music, to nature, to mathematics, to books, to the human body. It is a mathematical certainty found worldwide across all spectrums and fields. Do you think mere mortal men were smart enough to develop a system that identified all of it? *All* of it, with *no* divine inspiration whatsoever? I don't know about you, but I haven't met too many people that would even come close to being intelligent enough to turn the details of Earth into mathematical certainty from scratch. I'm certainly not a mathematical genius or any type of genius, but that seems a little far-fetched for me to believe that men came up with a formula that coincided perfectly with the whole universe by themselves. And we can't even count grains of sand! Do you want to hear a joke?"

"Of course."

"There's an old joke where a man challenges God that he can create his Earth from nothing, and God, amused, says, 'Sure, go ahead.' So, the guy reaches down to grab a handful of dirt, and God says, 'No, wait a minute, you have to make your own dirt too.'"

"I'll have to remember that one," Mattias said sarcastically.

I didn't slow down. "The total sum of humanity is just a germ on a skin cell of the human body in comparison to the totality of time and space, yet somehow, we developed conscious thought and intelligence and then presumed ourselves the great knowers of it all. That's the point I'm trying to make. *What if?*"

Mattias nodded, showing interest in my words. He was still keeping up with my logic, so I continued.

"Millennia of peoples since the beginning of time have all believed in something greater than them. Who are we to say all our ancestors since the beginning of time are wrong? St. Anslem of Canterbury said that the belief in a higher power should be enough to prove that one exists."

"That is all well and good," said Mattias calmly, "but there is still not concrete evidence of God himself."

"No, there is no family photo in a photo album anywhere, complete with His birth certificate, driver's license, passport, or social security card. Would anyone even believe it if there were, or would you say was all the documents were fakes? But that's the thing. I'm not asking you to believe me. I'm asking you to consider the '*What if?*' I'm telling you the straight truth, and the truth of my world. You're saying it sounds far-fetched and unbelievable, and your mind turns against it because it defies your logic." I pointed to my seagull, who was still standing a few feet away watching us.

"You say it's impossible, yet here we sit not ten feet away from a bird that's identical to the one in my picture. That's my story, and there's the seagull."

I looked out over the landscape, but I could see Mattias smiling in my peripherals. I couldn't tell if he was just amused, or if anything I had said was starting to sink in. I decided I had probably gotten too passionate and my tone had hit that fine line between inspired and stark raving mad. I determined that I had come across as a crazy woman, and he was deciding how to proceed.

I changed the subject. "Why did you bring me here, of all of the places? Why a road trip to the top of the world? Don't get me wrong. I've enjoyed it. I'm just curious is all."

"It is a long drive, but now you've seen a lot of Sweden's natural beauty. Peter said you appreciated uniqueness. I used to come here all the time, back when the world seemed simpler. I find the stillness to be reflective and calming. It's a unique peacefulness, sitting alone at the top of the world while knowing everything and everyone else is spinning beneath you."

I couldn't argue with that perspective.

Chapter 12

After we felt we had sufficiently experienced the beauty and nature which surrounded us, we started back down the mountain. I took a few more pictures along the way. I paused to catch my breath in a clearing overlooking a small mountain stream. I hadn't heard from Peter the whole week, other than a text asking me how I was doing. I looked at my phone. It was 7:00 a.m. If we left right now, we would get back around three or four a.m. tomorrow, and I might be able to get a quick nap before Peter came to get me. Mattias yawned. "I can drive part of the way if you'd like," I said. "I know you haven't slept in at least a day. I remember the way the last few hours. It was pretty much a straight shot. Just tell me what roads to look for, and then when we get closer to civilization, I'll wake you up and you can take over."

"That sounds like a fine plan, Cecelia. Thank you kindly."

I liked how Mattias said my name. He left one of the blankets out and wrapped himself up in it like a burrito before he sat down in the passenger seat. I turned the radio on, so low it was just a hum, to a channel that had light, easy music and climbed in the driver's seat.

I drove for about ten hours straight before we reached an area that looked familiar with buildings and hustle. Mattias had been asleep the whole time, lightly and peacefully snoring. I didn't mind. He had a quirky snore that made me giggle. Also, I knew that the poor guy was mentally and physically exhausted. After bearing his soul to me on top of the mountain, coupled with not sleeping for well over a day, I took a little pride in being able to take care of him, if even for a little while. I easily found the McDonald's we had dined in before, and I pulled into the parking lot. I gently woke up Mattias.

He looked slightly younger to me at that moment. Maybe it was the light, or maybe it was the rest he was getting. Instead of going Dutch as we had been, this time I treated him to a meal as a small way of thanking him for his time. I thoroughly enjoyed his company and the days we had spent together. As he drove the final leg of our trip back to Gothenburg, I noticed he had grown more silent, except for random anecdotes about various things we passed along the way.

I wasn't sure where we stood, if we stood anywhere. Maybe I was overthinking our time together. After all, we'd only known each other for a few days. Maybe he was thinking about what I'd said, or maybe he was just tired. Maybe he hated me and my beliefs. It wouldn't be the first time that had happened to me after I'd told someone about God and my testimony.

We returned to Mattias' house around six a.m., and he started cooking me breakfast. "Listen," I said, "I hope that you're not mad at me. I want to thank you so much for this week. I've honestly had the best time, and I enjoyed getting to know you. I hope that we can be friends."

His eyes crinkled as he smiled. "Why would I be mad at you, Cecelia?"

"When you were awake, you barely talked all the way back. In America, that's a bad sign."

"Ah yes, Peter told me about this. When he first moved to New York, it was the hardest thing for him to get used to. In Sweden, we keep more to ourselves. So, if we're around someone and are not talking, or long pauses happen without conversation, that's a sign of comfort for us. He said Americans constantly try to fill the silence. It shows signs of insecurity and uncomfortableness. So no, I'm not mad at you. I'm comfortable with you."

I smiled and let out a huge sigh of relief. My first few dates with Peter had made me feel so awkward in the silence when he would quit talking. "That makes me so happy! It makes so much more sense now. Peter hadn't mentioned that to me, but I wish he had. I was thinking about our conversation in the park, though. There are a few books I think you should read. They get into your brain and change the way you see the world, or they did for me anyway." "Give me a list, and I will look into them." Just then, someone knocked on the door.

Mattias went to open it, and there stood Peter. He walked over to me as I desperately tried to finish swallowing my eggs. I stood to greet him, and he kissed me long and hard. As I embraced him,

I glanced over and noticed Mattias was watching us, a saddened expression on his face. He was probably still tired from the long trip.

Peter turned around to him and said, "Thank you for showing Cecelia around. I appreciate you taking care of her this week."

"It was my utmost pleasure. I enjoyed her company more than she mine."

"I wouldn't be so sure about that," I said. "I had an incredible last few days. Thank you again so much for your kindness."

He put his arms around me and hugged me tightly. I held on tighter, for longer than I should have.

I heard Peter clear his throat before saying, "The driver is waiting. We must head back, Cecelia."

We let go, and my eyes looked up briefly to meet his. His expression was subtly different. I couldn't read it, but I felt as if he were trying to tell me something. I cradled his face in my hands and said, "Take care of yourself, okay?" He closed his eyes, nodded, and smiled.

On the plane ride home, Peter told me about all the success he'd had in the last few days. He was working as the liaison for the entire museum and had secured some significant exhibitions on loan. He had also acquired a few more permanent additions to several of the museum's areas, not just the photography department. Peter apologized again for having to leave, but he didn't stop to ask at all how my days had been.

After an hour of listening to him talk, I started telling him about my week. "I had the best time! We went to a rave, and we went to just about every McDonald's there is in Sweden. Then we drove to Abisko to watch the non-sunset. It was fantastic!"

Peter scrunched his nose. "He only took you to McDonald's?"

"No, he cooked for me quite a bit as well. A lot of local foods and delicacies. It was a lot of fun."

"I can start cooking for you too, if that is the sort of thing that you like. My brother can be a piece of work. He has always been footloose and fancy-free."

"I enjoyed him. He was a perfect gentleman and tour guide the whole time, and we have a lot in common. I think maybe you shouldn't be so hard on him."

"Did he tell you to say that? He makes me out to be the bad guy, when he's the irresponsible one."

"I think most people are fighting a silent battle, and you probably shouldn't judge them so hard if they don't live up to your expectations. Mattias is quite gifted and talented, but he's had a bad time of it. I relate, and I think it was good that we spent time together. I think it was supposed to happen."

Peter shrugged and ordered a gin and tonic. I watched the clouds go by until I fell asleep.

Back in New York, life resumed as usual, except that Peter had to be gone a lot more for work now. We grew a little more distant because of it. We didn't go to the Italian place quite as often anymore either. Instead, Peter insisted when he was home that he start cooking for me; but bless his heart, he didn't quite have the touch. Cooking is more of a feeling and an intuition, not so much a cut and dried process. Peter couldn't read a recipe to save his life, and most of the time we ended up ordering pizza instead.

He tried his best, and I couldn't fault him for that. There is nothing cuter than an adorable guy in the kitchen, towel over his shoulder, washing and scrubbing dishes encrusted in burnt food like there's no tomorrow.

We resumed our once-a-month dance classes whenever Peter happened to be in town, but I didn't seem to have as much fun anymore. It was the same routine, dinner and dancing. The most properly proper kind of dancing. Peter was sure of himself with scripted, serious, and steady movements, and we never danced closer than was appropriate.

I was keenly aware of my form and movements around Peter, honed into each and every minor hand movement and posture change. I mirrored his body language to feel more accepted, both by him and the company he kept.

I frequently prayed for Mattias and hoped he was finding his way. Peter didn't mention him, despite my suggestion that they keep in touch more often. Family is family, after all, and one only gets so many siblings in life.

I thought of our night at the rave frequently, how Mattias had been easygoing and unafraid of what he looked like to others. That night, surrounded by strangers, he had pulled me against his body. I remembered my head on his chest, listening to his heartbeat. At first it matched mine, but it had continued racing when mine had steadied with the pace of the music. His easygoing demeanor was night and day to Peter's pensive one.

I developed all the pictures I had taken and made duplicates of the ones from the mountain. Several of the best ones were of Mattias and me on the bench, making goofy faces or smiling. Some were just of him, and some he had taken of just me. I made duplicates of these as well and packaged them all up in an envelope. I wanted to send them to him, so he could see himself how I had seen him—beautiful and full of life.

I also included the one photo of the seagull. I wrote a short note thanking him for everything again. I wrapped it around the pictures and sealed the envelope. I texted Peter for Mattias' address and sent it in the mail that day. Months went by.

The gallery was doing well. I had finished all my previous commissions and lined up new ones. Roger kept promoting my gallery on his blog, but he was rarely in town. I didn't see him much at the dance classes Peter and I were able to attend, which took even more of the joy out of it for me.

Peter had lined up a few potential clients and treated them to dinner and a private showing at my gallery, which had produced several purchases. He had also called in some favors on my behalf, and several museums and galleries across the country started asking for me to loan them some photographs to display. I had sold most of my photographs, so I now focused on the ones from Sweden. I left the ones out of Mattias. That was a personal chapter that was his story alone. I included one of myself, just because I loved the mountainous scenery behind me in it, and the lighting made my eyes a deep green turquoise color.

Peter had started referring to me as his girlfriend since coming back from Sweden. We had broken down that wall somehow, but he still hadn't told me he loved me. Plus, he continued to not talk about the future. I didn't asked him about it either. I was so busy with the gallery and trying to keep up with my commissions. Touring the city and surrounding states for new material and opportunistic moments consumed my life. Peter and I were just comfortable existing together for a few hours a week out of our busy lives, and I didn't try to overthink it too much until I talked to Shelly a few weeks later.

It was October. Peter and I had officially been dating for a year, but I was no closer to feeling as if I was in love with him. Shelly didn't understand how we could be so nonchalant about our relationship, but I tried to explain to her that he was my best friend who occasionally kissed me. "We have great deep and mutual respect and support for each other. We share similar hobbies and have similar tastes in how we spend our time. We just have fun having fun without any pressure whatsoever. He's my rock and my support, and I love him for that."

Shelly sighed. "Blah, blah blah. He's sooo great and perfect and handsome, but you're not in love with him? That's so boring!"

Leave it to Shelly to cut through to the truth.

"No, I don't think so. I don't know. I only have Charlie to compare him to, and that was different. Peter seems distant a lot of the time. He almost constantly focuses on work."

"And he's successful and rich and sexy as all get out, but you *still* haven't slept together? And he's totally fine with it? You have *got* to be missing that part of a relationship. At least, I know I would. Maybe that's why you don't feel close to him."

"No, he hasn't asked or tried since that one night. We make out on the couch, which is great, but something is missing between us as people. I mean, I do miss that part, but it's not like that. I'm not that person, Shelly. You know this. I can't give my whole self to someone without knowing what I'll get in return. God doesn't want that for me, and I don't want that for me. I know I'm emotionally too fragile to just sleep with whomever. I don't even know if I want to get married again right now, or ever, but if I do, that's something I'd like to save for my husband. And I really don't know if Peter is that man."

"Fine, fine. Well, I'm just sayin' is all. You might need to think about letting him go then because that's not fair to him either."

Her words echoed throughout the night as I tossed and turned, flopping around like a dead fish and rearranging the covers constantly. I hadn't told her about Mattias in detail, only that I'd spent a week with his brother showing me around Sweden. I didn't know what to describe. Our conversations on the mountain? The music we shared? The way his eyes crinkled at the edges?

I felt as if there was nothing to tell, but everything to tell. I wanted my week with Mattias to be private, a secret that only we shared.

Maybe I could somehow protect him from the world so that he wouldn't be hurt anymore. It had been nearly four months since that week, but I still thought about him a lot. I missed being near him. I missed how he made me feel so welcome, so comfortable. I can't describe how good I felt around him. I didn't know why, but I felt like I was home. I didn't even realize how much I missed him. And I certainly wasn't even aware of how much I had been comparing him to Peter.

The day after my conversation with Shelly was a Friday, date day. Peter had decided he was going to try his hand at lasagna this time, which turned out to be a pretty decent, albeit ugly, meal. We scooped it into bowls and ate it with spoons, but it was delicious, and Peter was extremely pleased with himself after having so many failures.

I was about to ask him about our future, what he envisioned for us, and how he felt. I had been thinking about it a lot since the previous day, but he spoke first.

"I have some news you might enjoy. I must go back to Sweden next week for an extended weekend, and I wondered if you might like to join me? I will not make you any promises, in case something out of my control happens again, but I have already talked to Mattias, and he would be happy to host you, in case of emergency."

"Absolutely! Oh, that'll be so much fun! I've got a few free days next week, so that'll work out perfectly!"

I was so excited I could hardly contain myself, and Peter was grinning widely at my enthusiasm.

"This time, unless something happens, I will take you with me as I go to several of the museums, and you can fill your days running through the galleries." That did sound rather glorious either way.

The next week, it was like déjà vu all over again. The day before we flew out, Peter received a call from the museum. Where I had a layover in Berlin, Peter would have to stay behind. I would fly by myself to Gothenburg, where Mattias would pick me up.

Three days later, I would fly back to Berlin, where I would meet up with Peter and fly back home.

"This almost feels like a convenient little plot twist, Peter. Are you purposely trying to push me off on your brother?" I laughed, but Peter didn't laugh with me.

Peter looked at me, overly concerned. "I am not. I'm so sorry. I promise to you that it is out of my control. I can call and cancel your flight for you if you'd rather not go."

I wasn't worried, and I wasn't even a little upset. I was excited. "Calm down, it's fine. I was just teasing you. Mattias and I will have a splendid time, and I'll see you back in Berlin. Don't worry about me. I learned a little bit more Swedish the last few months, so I feel pretty confident I can at least navigate my way around the airport." He let out a small sigh, relieved that I wasn't upset with him, and he set my already packed suitcase by the door.

Chapter 13

My flight arrived in Gothenburg about thirty minutes ahead of schedule. I had remembered to get Mattias' number from Peter this time so that I could contact him myself instead of leaving the men to discuss and decide my fate amongst themselves. I texted him that I was there early and started toward the baggage claim. He did not text me back. I wasn't worried.

I took my time, stopping at the touristy souvenir stores along the way. I was looking for a lapel pin since I collected them from wherever I traveled. They were small, relatively cheap, easy to travel with, and pretty much any tourist destination carried them. Most airports did, at least. I selected one of the Swedish flag, one of the *Sailor's Widow* statue, and one of Abisko.

I made my way around to the baggage claim, checked which conveyor belt had my flight, and waited. It was located on the first floor of the airport, as it so often is. Not too far away was the platform where the taxis, Ubers, and pickups happened.

I buttoned my coat up. The wind from outside was making its way into baggage claim. I was looking super cute despite the cold. That morning, I had decided to fix my hair according to my excitement, and it stood as a blonde mane of curls around my face and on my shoulders. I had layered leggings under my dark blue skinny jeans, a tried and true method for me, with black calf boots. I also wore a white turtleneck sweater that was fitted in all the right places. My neck tends to get cold, and I'm always afraid a scarf is going to blow off, so turtlenecks are perfect. I had a three-quarter length tan puffy coat with a faux fur-lined hood that I'd bought on clearance several weeks earlier. Super chic.

I waited and waited for thirty minutes at least, but I didn't see my bag. It had traveled everywhere with me, including Sweden, the last time I visited. Purple with Hawaiian sea turtles on it, I had gotten it at the Hawaiian swap meet when I went to visit my aunt and uncle in Honolulu. I would be heartbroken if I lost it since it carried with it many good memories of my travels. It was unmistakable, but it was not here. Neither was Mattias, and I checked my phone just in case. He hadn't texted me back yet, and I began to get worried. Maybe my suitcase had gotten lost. Worse still, maybe something had happened to Mattias. I felt anxiety and uneasiness start to creep up in my stomach.

I started looking around for an airport attendant when someone tapped me on my shoulder. I turned around, and a gorgeous man stood there, holding my suitcase. "I believe these little turtles are yours?"

I blinked hard. He was the same tall man with broad shoulders, but gone was the man I remembered from months before. Mattias was wearing a tight-fitting navy-blue sweater and khaki pants, and I could tell what had been lean and skinny arms were now defined with enough muscle to see that he had been working out. He had put on about forty pounds, both in muscle and in body weight. His cheeks were no longer gaunt.

He looked ten years younger, but I still could see the precious crinkles at the corners of his eyes. Gone also was his thinning hair— he had shaved his head, and it looked great on him. He had even shaved his stringy, unkempt beard and replaced it with the perfect amount of light stubble. He was glowing, radiant to me, and I felt an adrenaline rush just looking at him. To put it simply, he looked like Christmas morning.

"Mattias! You look fantastic!"

He held out his arms for a hug, and I jumped into them and threw my arms around his neck. He held me tight against him. I was so happy to see him, and it felt so good to be close to him again. I hadn't realized how terribly I missed him, and tears started streaming down my face.

He laughed at me. "Cecelia, why are you crying?"

"I don't even know!" I did know. I knew I had been and was undeniably in love with Mattias Levander.

In the car, he said, "I have such fun things planned for you over the next few days. And I will not even make you go to McDonald's if you do not wish to. I hope you brought your camera."

"Of course, I did. Hey, did you get the pictures I sent you from my last visit?"

"Yes, I did. Thank you. The photos are beautiful—not the ones of me, but the ones of you and the scenery are beautiful."

I blushed and smiled. "You look amazing, like a different person from when I saw you last. What changed?"

"I changed. I am a different person. But I will tell you about that later. For now, we are on a time frame. We're on our way back to my house, where we'll change into formal wear quickly and head back into the city. I have a surprise for you that I know you'll love."

"What surprise?" This sounded exciting. "What requires formal wear? I didn't bring any formal wear. I'm wearing the fanciest thing I brought."

"No problem. When I found out you were coming last week, I sprang into action and enlisted my mother's help." Okay, I was super confused now.

"She is about your size, only slightly taller. She went shopping for you and found you a dress. *Turandot* is playing at the Gothenburg Opera house tonight, and I got us tickets."

I wanted to cry again. *Turandot* had been on my bucket list of things to see and experience. "How did you know I wanted to see that?"

"You mentioned it last time. You sang me a beautiful song from it, and I wanted you to experience it firsthand."

I had forgotten about that. "Mattias…I have no words. I'm speechless. I can't believe you remembered." Peter had certainly never done anything like this, and I was not used to it.

Mattias smiled broadly, his eyes lighting up and crinkling in the corners. I could have died right there at that moment.

"My parents have seats tonight too," he said. "Mom was the one who told me about it in the first place. We will find them after the show. They are excited to meet you. Mom got shoes and earrings for you too. She raised three sons, so she may have gotten carried away. She was overly excited to dress a female for a change."

My mind was racing. I had to press my ice-cold October hands to my bright red flushed face to calm myself down. Had he been this attractive last time? Yes, but I was with Peter, so I had tried not to notice it. Had I been this attracted to him the last time? Also yes, but again, I had tried to ignore it. Now, my heart and my mind were on fire for this thoughtful, sweet man beside me. I was a raging inferno of emotions.

I had not felt this alive with anyone since Charlie. I took a deep breath because I realized I was now also scared. Scared of what this meant, of what Mattias thought and felt towards me. I was still his brother's girlfriend after all, and Shelly's voice rang in my head from the weeks earlier. I knew I had to break up with Peter. It was not fair to either of us, especially if I was having these kinds of feelings for someone else.

I had tried last week to broach the subject. I should have tried harder. If I had, I would not be sitting here now. If I broke up with Peter and lost my relationship with both him and Mattias, I didn't know what I would do. *Everything happens for a reason. Just trust God,* I silently told myself over and over. I closed my eyes, took a deep breath and tried to calm my nerves.

Back at his house, Mattias acted like a perfect gentleman, unloading and carrying my suitcase into his bedroom. It was the same room I had been in before with the more comfortable bed, he'd said. This time it was different, more welcoming. The same lackluster décor, only this time on the bedside table, the lamp was removed and replaced with a vase of fresh-cut blooms. There was a beautiful multicolored arrangement of roses, peonies, irises, and a few other flowers that I knew weren't cheap.

Atop the table between the bathroom and closet were fresh fluffy towels and washcloths, and a small bowl of chocolates. A black garment bag, a shoebox, and a small jewelry box were laid out over the bed.

"What's all this?" I asked.

Mattias blushed slightly. "I wanted it to be nicer for you than the last time. I'll leave you to change." And he shut the door behind him. I was so excited I could hardly contain myself. He'd outdone himself with his preplanning. It was like a five-star hotel in here, and I was thoroughly impressed. I hung the garment bag on the front of the closet door and carefully unzipped it. A beautiful black evening gown came flowing out, and I held it up to admire. It was a strapless A-line, with a satin ivory band on top and layers upon layers of a flowing black chiffon skirt. Satin ivory long-sleeved gloves were draped around the top of the hanger, to accent the band. The outfit was exquisite, perfect for an opera.

In a plastic bag around the hanger was a tiny black satin clutch to hold the few belongings I needed to carry, such as lip gloss. I don't go anywhere without lip gloss. I noticed a shoebox on the floor next to the dress, and inside was a pair of three-inch satin heels that perfectly matched the two tones of the dress, black on top with ivory heels. They weren't so high that I would fall over, and I was grateful to Mattias' mom for considering that. Mom had chic and classy tastes, and I liked her already.

The earrings were equally timeless, pearls one on top of the other, with a black cubic zirconia diamond in between them. Also, inside the jewelry box were two hairpins, each with a pearl at the end of them as well. Mom had thought of the finest details and truly taken pleasure in this.

I went into the bathroom to refresh my face. I reapplied a little bit of foundation around my slightly tired eyes and applied some red lip stain to complement the dress and my eyes. I was so glad that I had left my hair down in curls, and I now pinned up a few select curls back from my face with the pearl pins.

I put my earrings on and applied a drop of perfume to my wrists and neck from a sample size of my perfume I kept in my suitcase in case of an emergency. I unzipped the back of the dress and climbed into it. The skirt of the dress was heavy and thick with the layers of chiffon so that it was not only beautiful but also highly practical in the October air.

It was tight-fitting around my torso, so I didn't need a bra. That was convenient since I didn't even own a strapless bra, let alone have one in my suitcase. My chest filled out all centimeters with no room to spare, but I still looked tasteful and modest. I tried to zip up the back, but despite my best efforts, I couldn't get my arms twisted around to reach the top half. Mattias would have to help me with that, and I put my shoes and gloves on and stood up.

In full opera regalia, I twirled in front of the bathroom mirror. The dress came just above my ankles and with heels on was just high enough so that I would not trip. I looked more like a blonde Audrey Hepburn than myself, and I held two fingers up to my lips, pretending to smoke from one of those elongated cigarette holders from the 1950s.

I exited the bathroom to find Mattias standing in the kitchen in a full tuxedo, looking out the window. "Darling, would you mind terribly zipping me up?" I said in my best Gatsby voice, turning my back to him before he could see me. I felt him find the zipper, and my breath caught in my throat at his touch. His fingers lingered on my back for a few seconds longer. He pulled the zipper up and fastened the clasp at the top.

I turned around, both of us seeing each other fully now. His eyes met mine. They were deep and longing and soft, and he said, "You look stunning, Cecelia."

Mattias' tuxedo was accented by an ivory tie and pocket square to match my dress.

"You're not so bad yourself." I felt myself blush deep red again. This wasn't going to be pretty if it kept happening against my red lip stain. I'd turn myself into a tomato face. I went to grab a napkin to wipe off the red stain before quickly applying the pink lip gloss from my clutch that was a closer match to my natural color.

"Shall we go?" Mattias said as he held out his arm.

When we arrived at the opera house, it wasn't what I was expecting at all. The only opera house I was familiar with was the one in *Phantom of the Opera*, huge and menacing inside, with large golden chandeliers and ornate gold decorations and statues from floor to ceiling. The Gothenburg Opera house was not even remotely similar. It was situated on the river, and its construction blended in beautifully with the surrounding ships and mariner landscape. Paned glass was floor-to-ceiling, and once inside, I could see that a restaurant was behind it. We walked over to the maître d, who looked up our reservation and promptly seated us.

This restaurant was upscale, fancier than anywhere I'd ever been, even in New York. Exquisitely dressed people were all around us, sitting at their fancifully laid out tables with wine glasses, gold cutlery, and white linens. No one noticed that I was not old money or new money. We blended in seamlessly. I couldn't decipher most of the menu, so I let Mattias order for the both of us. He picked two of the chef's specials, broiled lobster and squid in a white wine cream sauce with grilled vegetables and potatoes.

Our conversation over dinner flowed easily, as if no time had passed between us. I noticed Mattias ordered water for both of us, which surprised me. I had expected him to order some fancy champagne or wine to go along with the rest of the evening's mood. I remarked on the lavishness of the wine list.

"When last I first saw you, I had not had a drink in an hour. That hour has now turned to nearly five months."

I smiled at how he began the sentence so poetically. "You haven't had a drink that whole time?" I had to ask. Peter frequently had at least two or three drinks any time we went out, a fact that slightly irritated me even though I hadn't let him know it bothered me. Neither Charlie or I had ever made alcohol even a remotely occasional habit, and I didn't find drinking attractive at all.

"I promised you that I would not," he said pointedly.

I couldn't remember him saying he'd promised me, but I did remember him saying he had stopped drinking almost as soon as we'd met. I took it to mean he was trying to be polite, not that he was changing his habits for me. A stranger making that sort of commitment to another stranger would be too dramatic for anyone to achieve, so I had shrugged it off. Now I realized he had been serious about it, and I felt another surge of adrenaline at him keeping his word.

"I am so glad to hear that!" I said, nodding my head in approval. "I barely recognized you in the airport. You look so much healthier from when I last saw you. What changed?"

He was a little shy then and started fidgeting with his water glass. "I will tell you tomorrow. It is a long story for a different setting, and I want you to enjoy tonight at *Turandot.*" I was uncomfortably curious with all his mystery. "Well, it looks good on you, whatever it is."

We finished our dinner and walked towards the auditorium. Our seats were in one of the half balconies on either side of the stage. The auditorium was huge, as enormous as I had imagined it would be. The rows and rows of gold-covered balconies I had pictured in my mind were instead replaced with endless red rows as far as the eye could see. Three full red cloth-covered balconies rose above me, and a sea of red chairs lined the floor below me. From our seats, we had a full, close view of the stage, perfect in every way. We were so close I would be able to see the actors' facial expressions and emotions in detail, a beautiful element that gets easily missed with nosebleed seats.

"Do you know the story of *Turandot*?" I asked.

"No, I was looking forward to you telling me."

"Well, Turandot is a stone-cold woman with no love in her heart. In the final act, the aria 'Nessun Dorma' is sung by the prince trying to win her hand in marriage. She has made her courtship into a competition because she doesn't want to get married. He wins and counters her. He says if she guesses his name, he will die and she'll be free. In this song, the prince is basically saying no one can know his name. Oh, and she tortures a servant girl."

"I thought this was supposed to be a romantic opera."

"It is. It's in the music, even if you don't know what they're saying. It's one of the best-known arias in the opera world. It's going to be great! Just trust me."

"So how does it end?"

"I can't give you all the details. You'll have to watch and find out." I winked just as the lights flashed the five-minute warning.

The lights went out, and the curtain rose to reveal an elaborately decorated set and costumes from Imperial China, and I glanced over at Mattias. He had leaned forward in his chair, already intently captivated from the first opening scenes. We watched the elaborate costumes and scenery, conversing quietly back and forth about what was happening in each moment.

A little over an hour in, the prince began "Nessun Dorma," and we were both leaning forward intently in our chairs. I grabbed Mattias' hand and held on tightly, overcome with emotion. I mouthed the words perfectly and made a desperate attempt not to sing along and try to match the actor's pitches. The music echoed around me and throughout the auditorium, and I could feel my heart racing along with each note.

The entire crowd erupted into a standing ovation at the end of this aria, as clearly this was the crowd's favorite part. Mattias was on his feet, clapping and grinning wildly right along with me. "That was perfect!" I said. Throughout the rest of the opera, I was nearly in tears from excitement. When the entire cast started singing in the final scene, I lost all control of my emotions and began crying freely. As the cast took their final bow, the entire audience stood and started cheering and screaming in exuberance.

"What did you think?" Mattias asked after the cast exited the stage.

"It was all I ever wanted it to be! What did you think?" "Yes, it was not at all what I expected, and much better than I had imagined."

We waited for the crowd to clear out, and then we went back to the lobby to meet his parents. When Mattias said his mom was the same size as me only taller, I pictured three to four inches. Taller my foot, she was basically a Scandinavian supermodel. His parents were in their late fifties, early sixties, but I only knew that because of how old Peter was.

They hid their age well, and I knew where Peter and Mattias got their height. Their dad was easily six and a half feet tall; and their mom was probably six feet, or maybe even a little taller. I felt like Frodo when he arrived at the land of the elves. I was this short five-foot, four shrub surrounded by tall, beautiful Viking royalty. They both had golden blonde locks, and they both had cerulean blue eyes.

Peter strongly resembled his dad, but Mattias looked more like his mom. They were dressed superbly, as though they walked straight out of a *Vogue* cover. She had a few exquisite jewels on, and I noticed an elaborate antique emerald ring, an emerald pendant to match, and diamond drop earrings. I admired her tastes even more.

"Dear, it is so lovely to meet you," she said. "We have been looking forward to it after hearing so much about you. You've quite captivated our sons!"

"You raised fine men. Thank you so much for the dress and accessories! It's all so perfect!" I twirled around, gloved arms out to the sides to show her.

"You look astonishing, dear! I'm so happy I could help. Mattias has wanted to impress you for quite some time now."

I trained my questioning eyes onto to Mattias, who quickly said, "Okay, Mom, we should be going now." I had a feeling he cut her off before she said too much.

"I will talk to you later, Dad." They nodded to each other the way men do. His father had stayed silent other than saying hello, a typical man when the women get too chatty.

We went outside and walked along the waterfront for as far as we could. Boats were stationed all along the harbor, like tall looming skeletons. The night air was chilly, and as I shivered, Mattias took his tuxedo jacket off and wrapped it around my shoulders.

"Thank you," I said. "Thank you for everything. Your parents seem lovely and fun."

"Oh, that they are. They strongly support the arts and have season tickets to just about any theatre or venue they can get them for. I think that is the main reason our little brother is a stage actor. It's all he's ever known. He hasn't done opera yet, but maybe one day."

"Well, he should look into that. I'm so glad you enjoyed it. You know, Puccini never actually finished *Turandot* because he died. There's been a lot of controversy over the ending, and some people say it leaves much to be desired."

"Oh? In what way?"

"Turandot was so cold and horrible until she sees that Liu is in love with the prince. It doesn't make the music any less beautiful, certainly, but it leaves a lackluster ending according to a lot of people," I explained.

"I rather enjoyed it. The prince spent all of his time with the wrong woman."

"Yes, that's the story in one sentence." It was late, and I yawned somewhat loudly on accident.

"Yes, I think you're right. We'd better head home," said Mattias.

"Big day tomorrow."

"What are we doing tomorrow?"

"Another road trip! This one will be shorter than the last, I promise you. There is something I would like you to see in Norway since you appreciated the natural wonders so much on our last outing. We will spend the night in my cabin over there and come back the following day."

"I'm always up for an adventure."

We returned to his house around midnight, and I chuckled to myself that this time, midnight was pitch black.

I slept a deep and dreamless sleep that night and awoke at a decent hour the next morning, about eight. After a quick shower, I pulled my hair back into a ponytail. I chose jeans, a long-sleeved green sweater, double socks, and hiking boots for the day. I noticed any time Mattias mentioned natural wonder, that meant a lot of walking was included. I walked into the kitchen to find

Mattias once again cooking me breakfast. "Good morning," I said.

"Good morning," he said, smiling.

I pitched in to help with the morning's routine. We silently danced around each other in the kitchen as I gathered place settings for the table and poured us both glasses of juice and coffee while Mattias finished cooking. It was beautifully ordinary, the way we flowed around each other seamlessly without words or directions. I wouldn't have thought much about it except that I had not been in sync with someone like that since Charlie, and it made me smile. Mattias filled our plates with the all-American breakfast of bacon and eggs, and we ate in silence for the first few minutes. Mattias spoke first.

"Are you and my brother serious?" He had asked me this the last time I'd seen him. I wasn't expecting the repeated question, especially not right out of the gate today. I paused for a second, and finally decided there was no reason why I shouldn't be honest with him about Peter.

"No. I love him, I do. He's kind, sweet, and gentle. We have a lot in common and we get along great, but something is missing. I've tried to figure out what it is exactly, but there's just something about our personalities that doesn't quite click, I think. There's no reason why, other than we're just different people. He's been gone a lot of the last two months for work. We've barely even talked on the phone, and I only saw him once. Peter has modes. When he's in work mode, that's all he's doing, and there's no room for his personal life. When he lets loose, he's amazing, but I don't see that side of him very often."

Mattias nodded his head as I talked.

I was nervous about speaking the next words. "I've been thinking about breaking up with him, but I don't want to hurt our friendship…with Peter or with you."

I was stuck in a sticky situation, trying my hardest to show respect to Peter while he wasn't here, but at the same time not tell Mattias that I was desperately in love with him. I didn't want him to think less of me or get the impression that I was trying to be a brother hopper. I felt ashamed saying all of this to Mattias before Peter. Peter didn't deserve that. I wanted them both in my life no matter what happened.

"You will never lose me, Cecelia." He paused as if he were going to elaborate more. "My brother is professional above all else. That is the truest statement. What do you want? Who would make you happy?"

Who? Did I hear him right? I wasn't sure what he meant. Could he see my heart? Could he hear how loudly the blood was pumping through my veins right now? Did he know I was in love with him? Was he saying he felt the same? Or was he asking as a general question? Are we going to lay our love out right here over eggs and bacon?

I blushed a deep red, and my head was dizzy from my internal dialogue overreacting. I didn't know how to answer him, and I drifted sideways in my chair. I grabbed on to the table to steady myself, and he placed his hand on mine. I looked up and met his steady gaze, and he grinned at me as if he knew my secret.

Did he know? He must've known, must've heard my heart pounding out of my chest now.

"Are you ready to go on our next adventure?"

"Absolutely."

Chapter 14

Our car ride began much the same as last time. The first half of the trip was filled with Swedish radio, with a few stretching breaks between Gothenburg and Oslo. I noticed much of the landscape was changing as we drove. Norway felt more daring and dangerous to me. Gone was any semblance of the landscape I had seen before, replaced with towering, jagged, snow-covered mountains. Mattias turned the radio off, cleared his throat as if he were about to say something but apparently changed his mind. We rode in silence for a while, through the mountains and various towns.

Finally, he spoke. "Cecelia, when you last saw me, I was a different man."

"Yes." He had been a broken man, far more fragile than the beautiful hunk that sat beside me now.

"After we went to Abisko, I thought a lot about what you said. I thought you were crazy, Cecelia."

"Well, I'm used to that. Care to elaborate?"

"With your God, and your bird, and your books, and your analogies. It all seemed a little mad, but I couldn't get it out of my head."

"Thanks for not telling me this then. That would've put a damper on the trip. And?"

"And I started researching. I kept thinking about what you had said. *'What if?'* Such a simple question. What if there is something more, and everything does happen for a reason. Who am I to judge that? As you put it so plainly, I cannot even count the trees."

"Right."

"Right, so I started researching. I read every single theory out there, the Bible, the Apocrypha, and any other religious book I could find. Many of the world's religions are similar, have similar stories and themes."

"Yes, that's true. As you've discovered, many religions have similarities. There are many different accounts of Biblical stories across the board."

"Only the Christian God sacrifices His own Son," said Mattias. "To save humanity, yes, but why only this God? How do you know He is the real God?"

"Ultimately, we don't know yet, and we won't officially know until the day Jesus returns. No physical, tangible proof says, 'God was here,' and that's what starts a lot of the debates. We must rely on our understanding and our own experiences.

From my personal testimony, I have always had full faith in Him, and I have never been in any place, physical or mental, longer than I was meant to be. When I think back on my life, I can see each step and decision laid out so beautifully that I have no choice but to believe."

"Some books that say Jesus was not on the cross at all, that He was hiding behind a tree and laughing as He was crucified," Mattias said.

"His physical body was on the cross. His Spirit might very well have been watching from afar. As humans, we can't understand the spirit world. We can only make assumptions. Jesus' body died a physical, torturous death. He was mocked, beaten, and humiliated in front of crowds of people just because of his beliefs. Humans can understand, be afraid of, and sympathize with physical pain and mental humiliation. For a lot of people, the greatest fear is not fitting in with those around you, but Jesus was not afraid."

"So, Jesus died to make us uncomfortable?"

"In a sense, yes. To believe that Jesus is the Son of God is to put everything else behind you and acknowledge Him. Historians all pretty much agree Jesus was a great renowned prophet, but a lot of people have a much harder time believing that He is the Son of God. It takes nothing to be a ritualistic person, but to believe in the seemingly impossible demands a lot of courage and faith."

"And baptism is a representation of your belief? The Bible mentions it several times," Mattias said.

I answered his question with a question. "Is it enough just to make a promise to someone, or do you need also to fulfill that promise? It's the same thing."

I could see the wheels turning in his brain, but he was intently listening to my words. He said, "Jesus knew Judas would betray Him. Why did He keep him around? I read the gospel of Judas too, and it describes a very different world."

"Yes, Jesus knew the whole story before it happened. According to the gospel of Judas, he was the only one who, at the time, understood Jesus when He was talking about the spiritual world overcoming the physical world. This would've been hand in hand with the account of Jesus seen laughing at his physical body from behind the tree.

"A lot of the gnostic gospels were written centuries outside of the Bible for political purposes. You have to take most of them with a grain of salt and not read them as truth but consider that maybe they include truthful elements. Perhaps Judas had visions, like his gospel claims. We won't know the entire story while in our physical bodies.

"Modern-day people have visions and dreams all the time. You can believe that they're all crazy, or you can realize that they're all connected. Signs from God are all around us, you just have to pay attention. My favorite book of the Bible is Daniel because God spoke to him through dreams. In a way, I wanted to be like him when I was little, and as it turns out, I am. I had the courage to write Charlie that first letter based on a dream I had of him. I've had other dreams that influenced me also."

I hadn't told Mattias before about hearing his music in a dream, and I didn't tell him now. He had not commented much on his current beliefs, and I was afraid of him thinking I was even crazier than last time.

Mattias looked like the world was weighing on his mind. "I have had dreams since seeing you. I don't remember ever dreaming before you came, none that I could remember in vivid detail anyway." I turned my body towards him, as far as I could in my car seat, eager to hear more.

"Do you believe everyone has a soul?" he asked. "Even children and unborn children?"

"Absolutely I do. God creates us equally in His eyes, from conception, even if they are not born. Every soul matters to God."

"Where do they go if they are not baptized? If they do not know God?"

"They go straight back to Heaven because they do know God. Nothing is purer or more innocent than the soul of a child, and they are often sent to teach us lessons. Children are wiser than adults because they see things plainly, as they are and not what they want them to be."

Mattias pulled over to the side of the road and took a deep breath, as if he needed to concentrate. The tension in the car felt heavy, and I could feel he was about to reveal some soul-bearing revelation as he did on top of the mountain.

"I've had dreams every night, as clear as you are sitting in front of me. My son…" he began, his voice caught in his throat, "my son and I are playing in the snow, making snow angels. He has light brown hair, like mine used to be, and he looks a lot like me when I was a child. He is wearing a blue striped T-shirt and shorts, which I find odd because we are outside my house in Norway. It is the middle of winter, and I wouldn't let anyone dress like that, much less my own child. He sees me looking at him, and I've just figured out that I need to go get him a coat to protect him. He stops waving his arms and legs and sits up and looks up at me. He has dark blue eyes and he says, 'I'm okay, Dad. Do not be afraid for me.'"

Mattias was crying now and leaned into me, and I held him close for a few moments.

"I named him. I named him Greger. It means 'watchful.' I felt like I should name him. He needed a name, and seeing him each night, I felt like that was fitting."

"That's a perfect name," I whispered to him. He held on to me tighter. I wanted to tell him how beautiful he was, how dazzling his soul was, how much I was in love with him. Instead, I held him closer and cried with him there in the mountains of Norway.

Chapter 15

Driving across Norway made me a little bit dizzy at times, winding through the mountains with all the twists and turns. It reminded me of back home. Anytime we would vacation in Gatlinburg, Tennessee, we would decide to take the scenic backroads that usually ended up making us carsick. Despite that, it still felt like a necessary part of the trip.

When we finally reached our destination in Norway, we took or backpacks and boarded a ferry, which dropped us off at the base of a mountain located who knows where. All I could see were mountains, snow, and water. I had no idea in what town or location we were. All I knew was that I was in Norway. Being wonderfully lost in the wilderness, I realized all those people who talk about going off-grid might be on to something. This must be what it feels like to be only surrounded by the majesty of the outdoors. Not much civilization appeared to be here, other than the ferry and its operators.

Mattias explained that we were in a fjord, hiking straight up the mountain to an old farm called Knivsflå. From there, it would be just a little further to the top. When we reached the top, he hoped that our destination would be there. He hoped? What sort of adventure were we on? I could see a few scattered buildings in the distance above us and across the water from us. Mattias said the opposite side was an old farm called Skageflå.

In this cool wilderness, I breathed deeper and more thoroughly than I ever had. The air was pure up here, undisturbed by modern technology. It was different from the thick, sticky air in Savannah.

We were the only ones who had gotten off the ferry and the only ones on this hidden footpath as far as I could tell. It had not been used for a while, maybe months or years. Or maybe that was just how things looked in Norway, so well-built that everything withstood the test of time.

Some scattered patches of moss were visible where the snow was thinner. My boots crunched the tiny, fuzzy forests of earth as we started climbing.

"Typically, people do not come here at the end of October," said Mattias. "The season for fjords is in the spring and summer, when you can go kayaking and do far more hiking. Not fall and winter, when you can't feel your legs. It's too cold, and it scares away most tourists. But we're not just tourists, are we?"

I laughed. "Oh yeah, we're regular explorers." I was not as cold as I would've been had I not remembered to wear layers underneath my clothes—three layers each to be precise, strategically hidden so that I still looked cute while doing it. I had my tan coat on, hood pulled up over my head and fastened, plus an extra coat Mattias had hidden in his car. I was wearing extra thick gloves and a scarf that luckily I had packed last-minute, just in case.

Before we boarded the ferry, Mattias had pulled out of his trunk what looked like one of those suits people on Antarctica expeditions wear. He was quite puffy but quite adorable as he walked, a swishing sound made with each step.

"Do you know Pascal's Wager?" Mattias asked.

"Yes, either you believe in God and possibly gain everything and possibly lose nothing, or you don't believe in God and possibly gain nothing, but possibly lose everything. You can believe in something, or you can believe it's all just an accident."

"How did you come so easily to believe in God? If you had not met your husband, would you have believed?"

"I have found that a person's initial beliefs largely stem from where you're raised. Christianity overwhelmingly abounds in the South, so we are very familiar with it. Other parts of the country regularly make fun of the South. We're called the 'Bible Belt.' I believed before I met my husband. Had I not met him, I probably would've been baptized much later. God has a way of understanding us and our hearts. My parents did not regularly attend church, but I knew it was something that I wanted and needed to do, so I prayed about it. God sent me Charlie a short time later."

Matthias nodded, and I had the sense that he really felt and understood the depth of my words.

"I think there are a lot of situations where you may not be able to be baptized, but God knows the desire in your heart, and if your heart has truly changed, and He understands that. He knew us before we knew ourselves, and I think ultimately, He knows what's going to happen anyway. That's predetermination."

Mattias was deep in thought. "Mmm...you prayed about it? You regularly talk to God, and He's supposed to be listening? What if millions of people are doing that? He can't possibly listen to everyone at the same time."

I laughed, "No, maybe not. I like to think in scenarios, and I picture God sitting at a giant desk covered in yellow sticky notes of prayers that have come in. He gets to all of them, but maybe there's a secretary or two helping to keep all of the prayer requests organized. I've prayed for you too."

He stopped on the trail and turned to me. "You prayed for me?"

"Yes...I prayed for us. I thanked God for putting you in my life. I believe you are in my life for a reason that I do not yet know. But I am grateful to God and to you. You are precious to me, Mattias. Our friendship means a great deal to me, and I care about you deeply. I wanted you to be able to heal from your pain, to find happiness, and to find God." There, that was laying it out as plainly as I could without saying those other three words that were lingering on the tip of my tongue and my heart.

He looked at me, as he had that first night in the kitchen. Those dark blue, tranquil eyes stared right into my soul, and for a moment, I felt like he might kiss me right there on top of the mountain. I might let him. I had no willpower to stop him, not after we had exposed our souls to each other now. Instead, he broke his gaze and reached into his pocket to pull out his phone. He started scrolling through his photos.

We hiked on a little further, a little steeper, a little higher until we reached an old rustic farmhouse. It fit perfectly in this setting, with moss growing all over the roof. Mattias cleared some snow and debris off one of the steps, and we sat down for a break.

"I want to tell you something." I nodded my head as he continued. "I thought you were crazy last time, but you stayed in my head, and I kept hearing your voice saying, 'What if? What if, Mattias? Just free your mind.' I didn't start researching at first, either. It took a few weeks."

"What made you change your mind?"

"I came over to Norway and locked myself in the cabin for a few weeks longer to get away from life. Since rentals start slowing down the closer it gets to winter, I didn't have any bookings for a few weeks. I wasn't drinking. I just wanted silence. Peace to clear my head. But I noticed something after the first few days."

He held his phone over to me now, and I gasped, then smiled at the picture before me. It was a picture of a seagull, with a heart-shaped scratch on his beak and no right foot, sitting on a rail with a vast mountainous region behind him.

"I don't know if he was there the first few days. About a week after you left, I was outside on the deck, and he landed a few yards away from me. I ignored him at first. I noticed him, but it did not register in my mind that it was your seagull, and I went on about my business. The next day I was eating breakfast, he was still sitting on my deck, peering in. Again, I paid no attention to him until the third day when he was watching me from the rail, and I noticed he had no right foot. I gave him a piece of bread and went on about my business again. He was there for the few weeks that I was, looking in, taunting me, and I heard your voice again saying, 'What if? What if this bird is the Spirit of God?' I knew this bird was daring me. Stalking me."

I laughed again. "Maybe that bird was my prayers being answered."

"Maybe. So, I went back to Sweden after a few weeks. The very next day after I arrived, this very same seagull appeared on my deck in Sweden! Now curiosity had the best of me, and that was when I started researching. Right after I started researching, that was when the dreams of Greger started happening. As if it all was linked together, and God was trying to show me a path."

I smiled, warmed from the inside at where this was heading. "So, you believe God was showing you a path?"

"Yes, Cecelia. I believe in God. I feel as if He gave me no choice in the matter after meeting you."

I squealed with excitement, and I gave him a huge bear hug and kissed his cheek. The step we were sitting on was not the sturdiest thing, and it collapsed underneath the sudden movement. We rolled off onto the ground in fits of laughter. We tried to get back up, but we were both in so many layers that it was a futile attempt. We fell back down, side by side, and laughed even harder.

Mattias rolled over and propped himself up on one elbow. His dark blue eyes were twinkling, a light from inside illuminating his gaze. It took all I had to not kiss him. He looked at me, at my lips, as if he were about to, but he did not. My desire for him intensified.

"Thank you for seeing something in me worth saving when I could not, Cecelia."

Dear God, please let me have this man, I prayed silently.

The next few minutes of us trying to stand up while not rolling back down the mountain were worthy of a comedy show. Finally, we succeeded and moved further up. We hiked for about another thirty minutes before I started having a strange feeling.

By the sheer drop-off on our left side, I could tell that we were getting closer to the top. The trees started looking familiar, which was impossible because I knew I couldn't have been here before. I paused, and Mattias turned around to look at me.

"Are you ok?" he asked. "We can take a break if you need to."

"No, I'm fine. I have the strangest feeling, though."

"It might be the air. It is a little bit thinner here so high up."

"No, that's not it. It's like déjà vu almost."

We walked a little farther, and then I realized what felt off to me. I grabbed Mattias' hand and ran the rest of the way to the top, pulling him along with me. The scene was familiar, but not what I had seen before. "Waterfalls are here! Waterfalls are supposed to be here!"

Before us were just a few trickles of water, scattered out over the top of the mountain. The view was still exquisitely breathtaking, even in October.

"Yes, I had hoped the falls would be larger. They are called the Seven Sisters. In the spring, when they are full, it looks like the hair of seven women flowing down the mountain, but it is still beautiful in the off-season. How did you know what was here?"

"This is where I heard your music!" He looked stunned, taken aback by my words. "I heard it in a dream. I was here! Charlie and I were here, but he wouldn't talk to me. Instead, he just smiled, and I heard music playing—your music! The same day I met you! I haven't had any dreams about Charlie since that one!" My voice was nearly hysterical from excitement. This wasn't a coincidence. God had already answered my prayers before I even knew what to ask for.

As if in a romantic movie, Mattias turned to me and said, "The snow reflects in your eyes, gray-green. You are wondrous to me. You have seen my life when I could not, and you have felt my sadness across the sea."

"That's beautiful. Who wrote it?"

"I did."

I could read the emotions on his face like a book as my eyes looked deep into his with complete longing. My heart raced as he cradled my face in his hands and leaned down to kiss me. His kiss mirrored his eyes—deep, calm, yearning, and soft. I kissed him back with intense, furious passion. I wanted this man so badly. The cells in my body melted at his touch, and I felt my heart flutter uncontrollably. The last time I had seen Charlie in my dreams, he had not tried to catch me as I slipped off the mountain. He knew what he was doing; he always knew. I had fallen right here, straight into Mattias' awaiting arms.

Chapter 16

We spent a long time hiking back down the mountain, marveling at the majestic landscapes. The air was sharp and cold, but not unbearable until later on as the sun lowered. We had missed the ferry by the time we'd made it back, and darkness was falling. We were stranded in the middle of Norway and had to wait until morning for the next ferry.

We spent the night in a makeshift tent Mattias fashioned from the blankets he had stored in his backpack. They were large enough to block out the falling windchill, which was more prominent the darker it became. My backpack held protein bars, water, and matches, thank goodness, and we were able to build a small fire.

Being deserted in Norway for a night might have been an incredibly romantic situation if it weren't so cold. And if I didn't feel so guilty. We barely talked after the kiss. I was still trying to sort out what I was going to do, and what exactly it meant for the three of us. I took Mattias' silence to mean the same.

Later the next morning, on our way driving back to Gothenburg, my mind was racing. I was still with Peter, and I did not want to be duplicitous. No matter how much I had wanted to kiss Mattias—and I had desperately wanted to kiss him—I was not that person. I had kissed him in the moment, but I was sad about it now. I had selfishly prayed for this to happen, without thinking about the consequences or Peter's feelings. Mattias could tell I was in deep thought. I had grown noticeably quiet on the ride back.

As if he were reading my mind, Mattias said, "Cecelia, I am sorry. I was caught up in the moment and should not have done that. It was irresponsible of me. I know you're still with my brother. Please forgive me. I don't want to do anything to mess up our friendship." He had, though, and it was irreversible. Our relationship wouldn't be the same again. I did not want to hurt Peter, but I could not stay friends with Mattias. The wheels were in motion now, and I saw the events of the last year since meeting Peter laid out before me so clearly now. I stared out the window, counting the tops of the mountains.

"That's the thing about the past," I finally said. "When you look back, you can see all the decisions that led you to where you are today. All it takes is one person to say or do the right thing and change your perspective, and then you see the world differently. You can see God through the events in your life, and that's the clearest way to see reality."

"Cecelia? Are you mad at me?"

"No, Mattias. I should not have kissed you, though. I don't regret it, but it was wrong to happen while I'm still with Peter."

"You don't regret it?"

I hesitated. Should I tell him how I was feeling?

"No, not at all." Maybe he could hear my heart beating out of my chest. I was pretty certain all of Norway could hear it. I could feel the tension in my body start translating itself into a pounding headache.

"Your heart is not with him?" he asked as if to be sure.

"He doesn't know that, and I'm not that person. I can't be that person."

Mattias nodded. I felt as if he understood everything I said before I had even said it. I'd felt that way since we first met. So much was unspoken between us, but I was sure he was in tune with my emotions.

He tried to change the subject, to go back in time to yesterday. "If God gives us free will, what is the point of creating us in the first place? He could tell us what to do, and problems would resolve themselves without pain and suffering."

"Authors have described creating their characters as an in-depth journey into their soul. They are responsible for these characters' feelings, thoughts, and ideas as they seek to make them all individual, unique personalities. If we were just God's puppets, and if He did not create us as unique individuals, what would be the point? I like to think of us as a science experiment, as if God is in high school. It's funny that way, as if He's watching us mess up and writing papers on it. The same way we watch sea monkeys and fish aquariums. Maybe we're just like a bunch of sea monkeys."

"I am not familiar with sea monkeys."

I giggled at his frankness. "They're a type of shrimp, very tiny and easy to grow. Sea monkey aquariums were extremely popular when I was little, but I was the only kid I knew that didn't have one. Mama said it was cruel to keep them. They're kind of sad and creepy, these little things stuck in a bowl with no life or fun or free will at all. If we didn't have free will, there would be no point. And God gave us a much nicer habitat than a bowl.

"If there were no point to anything, there would be no reason for moral laws. C.S. Lewis said since moral laws exist, then there must be someone who made the moral laws. If there were no God, and we did not believe in punishment, crimes would no longer be crimes."

"Moral law, like it is wrong for one to whisk his brother's girlfriend away on a romantic adventure and then kiss her?"

I smiled at his reasoning. "Please, Mattias, honestly, it's okay. Don't beat yourself up. I was there too, and I kissed you back. I should have broken up with Peter weeks or months ago, but if I had, would any of this have happened? If I hadn't had that dream, would you have still kissed me? I want to be honest with you. To do that, I also must be honest with Peter, and he doesn't deserve this."

"I understand. I will say no more about it. The theory I fell in line with the most was John Hicks'. Do you know it?"

"I've heard of him, but I can't place him right now."

"Hicks came up with what he called the 'soul-making theodicy.' In his theory, he explained why evil is present, saying that we were all born unfinished, but our earthly lives toughen us and make us who we are supposed to be, which is how the world got to be where it is."

"Free will, in other words."

"Yes, all of the things you've been saying and that I've been feeling. Viewing my life like that helped me to answer my questions and find peace within myself. That was when I started taking better care of myself. I have no one to blame any longer."

"Mattias, I am so proud of you and how far you've come. I want you to know that." He opened his beautiful lips to speak, but then thought better of it and remained silent.

We arrived back in Gothenburg just a few hours before my flight left. We stopped at his house to pick up the rest of my things that I had left behind and then went straight to the airport.

"I need to tell you," Mattias said, "I plan on being in New York in a few months. I have been sending out feelers for galleries, and I have an appointment with one gallery in New York in January."

"Oh! That's fantastic! Wait! I have an extra bedroom. Don't book a hotel or anything, stay with me!" I'd spoken before I'd realized how awkward it might be. It was a tad bit forward of me to offer, but it was the least I could do to repay his generosity. He had, after all, set aside plenty of time to show me around Sweden. He looked at me, his brow slightly furrowed, and his eyes were squinting in curiosity.

Then he smiled happily.

"That would be kind of you."

"Please, it's the least I can do, and we're friends, after all, right?"

"Forever. Please keep in touch, and I will let you know the exact dates." We hugged for a long time. I didn't want to let go. He smelled of fresh air and hope for the future. A tear slid down my cheek, and he wiped it away. He leaned in and kissed my forehead. "I will see you soon, Cecelia."

Chapter 17

Waiting to board the plane I was nervous, anxious, and worried.

My heart was sitting in my stomach. What if it was all a mistake? What if I was doing the wrong thing and had just been caught up in the moment? What if I lose Peter and Mattias? I didn't think I would lose either of them, but I couldn't be sure until I moved forward.

And I had to move forward. I knew that I was in love with Mattias, and I was now almost certain he was also in love with me. I should have been honest with Peter long before now. Why wasn't I? I didn't consider myself a cruel person, but my nerves churning around in my stomach now made me feel otherwise.

I could imagine my life before me, taking two paths. A life with Peter would mean endless parties and events, infinite travel and museums, and shaking hands with the highest members of the art society. It would be a glamorous, prestigious career and lifestyle for any photographer or artist. But even Frida and Diego were miserable. They had the marriage, the artistic career and lifestyle, the money, the notoriety, but still it wasn't enough to keep them personally satisfied with each other.

I imagined myself in beautiful gowns, attending the Met Galas, but always ending up alone while Peter was off galivanting with the next big client. I imagined my days long, lonely, and full of outward perfection from every angle.

A life with Mattias I envisioned much differently. I imagined several children, the both of us only working when we wanted and possibly even sharing a gallery. I remembered when I fell asleep in his arms that night in the tent when we'd missed the ferry. I wanted more of that life. I could easily see myself falling asleep in his arms for the rest of my life, listening to his adorable little snore and seeing him smile as he slept—such a simple and happy life filled with each other's company. Being with Mattias, no matter where we were or what we were doing, had proved to be calm and blissful. In my mind, he represented being far away from the chaos of modern society, with all its expectations and letdowns. I wholeheartedly knew who my choice was. About an hour outside of New York, I worked up the courage to talk about it.

"Have you ever been in love with me?" I asked suddenly. I meant to be more tactful about it, but my nerves made me blurt it out in the open.

Peter looked at me, his ice blue eyes wide with shock and alert.

He put down his magazine. He opened his mouth to speak and said, "Cecelia-."

My stomach was in knots and I interrupted him. Again, tactless. "I've been thinking a lot over the last few months. I want to say first and foremost that I do love you, and you're my best friend. I want you in my life always, but I think that we should see other people. I don't feel like we have the romantic connection that we both deserve."

Peter looked at me, a shocked and saddened expression across his handsome face. "Why are you feeling like this? You haven't said anything before."

"We're constantly busy, and it just doesn't come up—me with the gallery, you with your work. We have a great time when we're together, but that's only once a week, if even that. I hate to use a horrible cliché, but here goes. I love you and care for you deeply, but I'm not in love with you."

"Help me understand."

"We get along fabulously, and we enjoy each other's company. I do value and care for you as a person and for our friendship. But it's not deeper than that. It's never felt like anything deeper than that, on a romantic or spiritual level. Peter, we've been together for nearly a year, and you haven't said you loved me. We haven't talked about the future, not once. You've never even mentioned anything about the future or seeing me in yours. We haven't even talked about anything serious regarding the two of us."

"You needed time to heal."

"I did need time to heal, and I needed support and patience and kindness—all of which you provided me, and I love you immensely for that. But now I need more, and I don't think I can find it in us." I was almost in tears. I hated these words that were coming out of my mouth, and the look of sadness across his handsome face, but I knew he was not the one for me.

"Is this why you didn't want to be intimate with me? I tried to let you have your space, should I not have?"

"Only a few months ago did you even start calling me your girlfriend. Peter, I need more now. I want a future with a man who wants to make time for me and put me first. I can't just sleep with someone I'm not serious about, who doesn't see me in his future. I can't just give that part of myself over. I'm not a modern girl. The only man I've ever been with was my husband, and if I'm ever with someone again, it's going to be for life. I am solid in that.

"You're so busy with work. Please understand I'm not blaming you or saying anything is your fault. I'm just at a point in my life where I'm ready to move forward, and I don't think you're the one I can move forward with. I don't even know if you're at that point because we don't talk about it. Are you even in love with me, or are you just comfortable with me?"

He just looked at me, still quiet.

"Are you even in love with me?" I repeated. "Were you ever in love with me?" My voice was showing irritation. "Peter, honestly, I don't understand you most of the time. You're so confusing to me. You're so serious all the time. You rarely let your guard down, and I feel like you've never let me into your life. Not fully.

You've kept a wall up this whole time that you won't let down for anyone, not even for me. That is where all of this is coming from. Why did you even take me to Sweden? Why did you take me back to Sweden a second time?"

I didn't give him time to answer. "I met your parents this time, and they're complete angels. Your mom bought me a dress and shoes. I've spent more time with your family, by myself might I add, in the last six months than I have with you. That's not a great foundation for a relationship. I know it's not your fault that work pulled you away, but the fact remains that you had to put work first. I had to get pushed to the side, and that has happened a lot at home too."

Peter's voice was frustrated now. "And I have put your gallery first many times. I have gotten you commissions and clients and loan agreements from museums across the country. I thought you would enjoy time away in Sweden, so I took you. You enjoyed it so much the first time, I took you back for a return trip. I didn't mean to leave you alone either time, I wouldn't have done that on purpose. We had an understanding that there was no pressure on our relationship and that it was not a formal agreement."

"A formal agreement? What does that even mean? Yes, you put my gallery first many times, and I appreciate you for that. What about me? We don't really have a relationship but a friendship between professionals who occasionally make out and go to dinner on Friday nights."

We were both getting flustered. I sighed heavily, sad and frustrated at where this had gone.

"That is what I mean. I need more than that now. I don't want to argue with you, and I don't want to fight. I don't want us to be mad at each other. I like our Friday nights, but I need someone who can be spontaneous and go out on a Monday night as well. Peter, I do love you, but I am not in love with you. Please understand where I'm coming from. Maybe we could've had that moment a long time ago, but frankly, you were very hard to figure out and understand and I wasn't in the emotional mindset to try." I hated myself for resorting to clichés.

"I am healed now. You are my best friend and my rock and my support system. You mean more to me than you could ever know, and I do not want to lose you in my life. I still want us to talk and watch movies and go to dinner. I want all of our friendship, but I need someone in my life who is emotionally available to me seven days a week, someone who doesn't just pencil me in on Fridays from five to ten p.m. I think that we should be free to see other people and not have to feel guilty about it is all I'm saying. This relationship, us as a couple, there's more to be desired for both of us and we should find what we're both looking for. "

He cut straight into my heart with his next words, like he already knew what had been quietly happening. "Who are you wanting to be free to see?"

He looked away from me, towards the front of the plane. I saw a sadness on his face I hadn't seen before, but I needed my feelings to be out in the open.

"I want you to find happiness with someone who loves you fiercely. Peter, please don't be mad at me. I couldn't stand it if you weren't in my life anymore. But I think this is the best for both of us."

His voice showed no emotion now. "As you wish."

We shared a taxi back to my gallery, and we did not talk the entire way. My heart was pounding in my chest. I was attempting to maintain my composure and not cry in front of him. When the taxi stopped in front of my building Peter finally spoke, his voice soft.

"I gave you enough space so that you could be free to heal and be with me when you were ready. I wanted you to choose me because you wanted me, not because I was there." I stayed silent, my heart shattering inside. If he could have opened up like this after we'd first met, things might've turned out very different.

We both stepped out of the car, and Peter unloaded my suitcase. I tried to hug him, but he evaded me and got back into the car. A cold, sharp wind whipped through the air, and I felt it slice between us. He was avoiding me now and wasn't even looking at me as he sat there.

"Peter, we'll talk soon, right?" My voice was higher and strained.

I was worried, and tears started trickling down my face. "Peter?"

"Yes, Cecelia. Goodbye."

I barely made it up the stairs. Before I could open my apartment door, I collapsed in sobs onto the landing.

Chapter 18

I didn't hear from Peter that week, or the next week, or the week after that. The silence was deafening, breaking my heart with each passing day. I missed him immensely, and I wasn't entirely sure if I had done the right thing. I missed the way we fit perfectly together on his little blue scooter, and how he made me laugh because he was overly serious about the stupidest things. I missed how his handsome face scrunched up in defeat when he inevitably burned whatever food he was cooking, and how when we danced, his tall frame was so steady and commanding.

I missed how he pronounced Swedish words to me, slower so I could comprehend them with my American ears and attempt to repeat them back to him. I missed our dinners at the Italian restaurant, and how his favorite part was the tiramisu. When the waiter would bring it, Peter would get this silly grin as if he were at Disney World, and it was the cutest thing.

I missed how he smelled like new books, and how he had had a raindrop on the end of his nose the first time I'd seen him. I tried to call him after the second week, but it went straight to voicemail. I had cried myself to sleep that night and for the rest of the week.

I had not heard from Mattias either, which didn't necessarily worry me, but I felt I should at least check in with him. Three weeks after I broke up with Peter, I worked up the courage to text him that I had done so. He replied shortly thereafter, asking if I was okay. He gave me the dates that he would be in New York. It would be the middle of January, the coldest time.

The following week I tried calling Peter again on a Friday, to see if he was available. It was dance night, maybe we could dance the distance between us away. He answered this time, short and cold.

"No, Cecelia, I will not be going." And he'd hung up.

I called back, angry this time at his childish conduct. Straight to voicemail. I sent him an angry text saying that he needed to quit behaving like a child and start acting like my friend. I received no response. I did not call or text him again, and he made no efforts to contact me.

Two and a half months later, Mattias flew into New York. On that Friday, it was snowing outside. I had sold most of the Life and Death gallery, and most of my other random photos. Now my pictures of Sweden and Norway hung on the walls, graced by a few before-and-after pictures of Mattias. After keeping them to myself for so long, I had decided finally to include them in my gallery. He was so handsome, and I enjoyed seeing him, smiling at me with the crinkles in the corners of his eyes. It made me immeasurably happy, and I felt safe and protected.

Peter had not been anywhere close to my gallery, which was a good thing. I had made no mention of how close my friendship with Mattias had grown. He would've been furious if he had walked in and seen his brother plastered on my walls. I had a few clients throughout the day, but my mind was focused on Mattias.

It was difficult for me to be patient, to barely have any contact with either of the brothers, not knowing how things would play out. Mattias was supposed to be flying in on Sunday. His appointment was on Monday, and he would fly back out on Tuesday. It wouldn't be nearly enough time with him, and I missed him already. Our kiss played over in my mind every single day. Thinking about being in his arms made me feel happy, calm, and alive. I missed him even more.

I was changed with Mattias, as though our spirits had found each other after a long journey apart. I had known him, loved him in another world, if ever such a thing existed. I knew my heart was safe with him, as if our souls had already joined to form one person.

I was lost in my daydreams when I heard the antique bell ding, followed by some crunching of bags and shuffling. "What on earth is that?" I muttered quietly to myself as I felt the blast of January air rush in and all my expensive heat rush out. I walked around the corner and squealed with delight. Carrying several grocery bags of food as well as his suitcase was Mattias.

"Hey! Cec—" He didn't have time to form a complete sentence before I rushed into his full arms. He dropped the bags on the floor and held me close.

"You're early! You were coming on Sunday!"

"Oh please, that would never be enough time with you, Cecelia. I've missed you so much. I bought groceries so I can cook dinner for you tonight. What time does your gallery close?"

"Right now!" I rushed to flip my open sign over; it was almost closing time anyway.

"You look as radiant as ever, Cecelia." I was wearing a cute full-length floral dress, yellow with pink, white, and teal flowers. It had capped sleeves, which were so adorable that I didn't wear a sweater with them. I had the heat turned on high enough that I was fine. It didn't matter one bit that Mattias had just let all that heat out. I was so flushed with excitement that I could've stood outside in a bikini for hours. I gave him a quick gallery tour, pointing out the photos that meant more to me.

"Cecelia, I was not aware that I was all over your walls. I feel a little awkward, staring at my past self." Mattias grinned at me.

"I think it's wonderfully inspiring. I'm so proud of you, and I wanted my clients to see your transformation, to feel how far you've come." We picked up the groceries and his suitcase and went upstairs.

"Shall I start cooking?" he asked after I gave him a quick tour of my apartment and let him settle into the guest room.

"Absolutely. What will the chef be preparing tonight?"

"I thought you might like snow crab with fettuccine Alfredo, with mushrooms and asparagus."

"I would indeed!" I didn't have to point anything out. Mattias glided around my kitchen as if he had been there before, familiar with each pot and utensil I possessed. It was funny how we fit together like a zipper, with no part left unconnected to another. I wanted to tackle him, to kiss his sweet face until it was time for him to leave, but instead, I just flushed bright red again and said nothing.

I sat at the island, watching him work and trying to contain my happiness so that I didn't come across as gushing.

"Do you have a record player?" he asked.

"Yes, it's over there by the window."

"That's good news. I brought you something I think you'll like."

I grinned as I watched him float around my kitchen. In just the short time I had gone without seeing him, I had missed him even more than before. I was so thankful that he arrived early so we would have more time to spend together.

"I have three meetings on Monday with several galleries," he said. "None of them are the Met, though. Have you talked to Peter?"

"No. He won't talk to me. He was angry with me when we got back, and he shut me out. I tried calling him, but it goes straight to voicemail," I said.

"He doesn't know that I am in town unless Mom told him. I sent him inquiries for my works, but he didn't respond. I guess he wants me to find my success over here and not ride on his coattails."

"Well, forget him. I have connections if you need them, and you can use some of my wall space if you need to." I told him about Roger and his vast network of associates, and how he'd probably be more than happy to help get a gallery show going on and advertise on his blog for a small fee.

As the aromas in the kitchen grew more pronounced, I started setting the table. I decided against lighting candles. I didn't want to seem too forward, even though I was desperate to tell Mattias how I felt. I could hear Shelly's future voice in my head if I lit them, saying, "I can't believe you lit candles! How presumptive of you!"

Either I was right and he'd think it was romantic, or I was wrong and it would be more awkwardness than I would be able to recover from, I was certain. I was also fairly sure that I wasn't crazy and that he did have feelings for me—but better safe than sorry.

By the time I had set the table, he had not only plated the food already but had also quickly washed all the dishes. He was too good to be true. He brought the plates over to the table, then disappeared into the guest bedroom for several minutes. When he came back out, he was grinning and holding a record.

"What's that?"

"This! A gift that I had to search far and wide for, the original recording of *Turandot* starring Luciano Pavarotti."

I was dumbfounded. "You found that? I didn't even know it still existed outside of YouTube!"

We ate dinner while listening to it, and I explained which songs correlated with which parts of the imagery from our night at the Gothenburg Opera. The evening replayed in my mind, thinking about how cute he had been as he leaned forward with his brow furrowed, trying to figure out what was going on before I could tell him.

When we'd finished eating, Mattias stood and turned the lights out. He walked over to me and held out his hand. "Would the lady care to dance?"

I took his hand, and we walked over to the space by my front windows. Snow lined each pane of glass, illuminated faintly from behind by the streetlights. He whispered a few lines of a poem to me as we swayed gently.

"Who is that by?" I asked. I had heard it before.

"Robert Louis Stevenson, a poem called 'Duddingston.'"

"Ah yes, he's an old friend of mine."

He looked at me with a questioning look in his eyes.

"In Savannah there's a restaurant called the Pirate House. I've had many a meal there. It was an old tavern back in the day, and it inspired him to write *Treasure Island*."

He pulled me close to him, like we had danced that first night at the rave when we were so familiar and unfamiliar at the same time. I rested my head on his chest, listening intently to his heart. It was racing furiously, the same as mine, despite swaying slowly to the music. *God, please let me keep this man. I have to keep this man,* I silently prayed to myself.

"Nessun Dorma" started playing, with Pavarotti's deep voice echoing in surround sound throughout my apartment. It couldn't have been any more perfect or romantic, Life was about to change. I could feel the atmosphere adjusting around me with each passing note and step. The snowflakes landed on the windowpanes in slow motion as the hairs on my arms tingled. I could faintly see my breath against the streetlight as Mattias held me tighter. I could feel that he was as deep in this moment as I was. As the song came to its final epic moment, I couldn't maintain my composure any longer. I looked up into his eyes, and he looked down into mine. Without a word from either of us, only Pavarotti narrating our moment, our lips met quickly, furiously like two magnets being drawn together.

I kissed him freely, as a single woman without the shame I had felt before. He cradled my face in his hands, I loved it when he did that, and kissed me back with ferocious intent and purpose. My heart, my stomach, all my organs melted into butter, and each cell in my body exploded again as they had that day at Seven Sisters.

My hands started shaking in excitement, and I wrapped them around his neck and pulled him closer to me. I felt a tear flow down my cheek, and when he felt it, he pulled away.

"Cecelia, I am in love with you. I've been in love with you since the first moment I saw you by the window."

"I'm in love with you too," I said as I pulled him back toward me and kissed him again. We swayed together long into the night, with nothing illuminating us but the streetlights.

We managed to part early enough so that we could try to go to sleep at a decent time. I knew Mattias was exhausted from the flight, and I now had plans for us that started somewhat early in the morning. We kissed goodnight and went into our separate rooms, but I was on fire for hours. He had said he was in love with me, and we had finally reached that moment, which if I was being honest with myself, I had wanted almost immediately after meeting him.

Mattias was no ordinary man, and this was no ordinary love. This profound and passionate affection and desire between us had blossomed from the things I held dear to me. I paced around my room. I wanted him so badly, but I couldn't sleep with him, could I? No, I couldn't. That would make me a liar to Peter and go against my moral beliefs. I wasn't good at dating. I didn't know how to date at all. What came next? What should I do?

I had been married to Charlie early on, and then there was Peter, and that was the extent of my dating experience. I knew I was overthinking. I had only ever been a wife, and I didn't know what the next step would be. I believed Mattias was my future, but I was not going to sleep with him. But I wanted to. I paced more furiously, giving myself a headache with all my questions. I probably shouldn't try to plan out our future just yet. After all, he had only just told me he was in love with me. That kiss was electric. I could still feel him on my lips, and I wanted more.

I made up my mind. I was going to march over there and tell Mattias exactly what I had told Peter months before, that I would not sleep with anyone until we were married, and that included him in all his handsome, breathtaking glory. He could take it or leave it. No matter how much he kissed me or cooked for me or made me listen to *Turandot*, I was sticking to my principles. It was early on, so if he wanted to dump me after one night, then so be it. I'm strong, I've recovered before, and I'll recover again. I made myself already mad at him in the scenarios in my head, to help me recoup better if it went sideways.

I stomped over to my bedroom door, threw it open, and almost fell backward with shock. Mattias was already there leaning against the door frame with an amused expression on his face, apparently listening to me pace around.

"I can't—"

"I know," he said, cutting me off as he wrapped his arms around my waist and pulled me close, "but I wanted to kiss you again." In the doorway of my bedroom that night, I knew my heart was safe.

Chapter 19

I woke up early the next morning to the smell of bacon and cinnamon. "This man cannot be real," I whispered to myself as I went in the bathroom to wash my face and make sure I looked halfway presentable. My hair was a mess, so I pulled it up loosely in a messy bun. I brushed my teeth quickly. Many women have tried for millennia to give the illusion that we do not have morning breath, and I wasn't going to let us all down now.

My pajamas were cute enough and didn't make me look like a puffy marshmallow person, so I proceeded on. I walked into the kitchen, where Mattias was icing a pan of cinnamon rolls. I took a moment to just look at him. He was so adorable. He had blue flannel pajama pants on and a plain white undershirt that showed off his muscles.

His expression was super serious as he was icing, and he only noticed me when he turned around to the sink. I wrapped my arms around his waist, "I love that you cook, did I ever tell you that?"

"I love that you love that I cook."

I slid around, under his arm, and put myself between him and the sink. He kissed me softly. "I love that you kiss me," I said softly.

"I love that you love that I kiss you," he whispered in my ear before kissing my neck, face, and lips again. We were adorably disgusting. I could've stayed in that moment forever.

As I was pouring us some juice, we heard a knock on the door.

"Expecting someone?" said Mattias.

I looked at the clock and saw that it was 8:00 a.m. "No, it must just be the mail coming early today because of the weather." I walked over and opened the door slightly. Peter stood there, looking frazzled and exhausted, as if he hadn't slept in weeks. His usually slicked-back golden hair was messy and wild.

"Peter, what are you doing here?" I said.

"Can we talk? I need to talk to you, Cecelia." I pulled the door back towards me so that it was only open the width of my body, and he could not see inside. "No, Peter, it's not a good time. We can talk later in the week, okay?"

"It was the alfredo!"

I was extremely confused. "Huh? What're you talking about?"

"That was the moment I knew I was in love with you. On our first date, you ordered chicken alfredo. As you were eating it, just a drop of the sauce splashed up on your nose. I didn't have the heart to tell you. You were trying to be so serious with me but all the while you had sauce on the end of your nose. You want stories like that, details right? The why and the how, that speaks to you. I get it now." He was trying too hard, being too vulnerable and uncharacteristic.

At least I knew now that our first dinner had been a date after all.

"You were *right*, Cecelia. I *should've* made more time for you and put you first." His usual carefully constructed speech contained more feeling than I'd ever heard him speak. "I'm too uptight. I've been too uptight, but I should have told you how I felt. I *am* in love with you, and I *do* want to marry you. I will marry you, Cecelia. Will you marry me?"

I stood there with my mouth open slightly, trying to understand what he'd just said. My heart broke for him, for the answer I knew I would give him. "Peter, we should talk about this later. Now is really not a good time."

Just then, Mattias dropped something into the sink. It made a soft clinking sound, but it was loud enough to hear. Peter's face changed from desperate to serious in an instant.

"Is someone in there with you?"

A fleeting look of guilt swept over my face, but Peter caught it.

"Is someone in there with you?" He repeated himself more forcefully this time.

"Peter, this is not a good time. I'll see you later, okay?"

He pushed the door open. Mattias stopped what he was doing and looked up at us. I looked back at Peter in the doorway, whose ice-blue eyes had widened in recognition before exposing his fury.

"You!" Peter screamed.

"Peter, go away. We will talk about this later!" I tried to block him with my short frame, but he was too big for me. He marched right past me and barreled towards Mattias, who was almost to us now.

Poor thing, he didn't see the first blow coming as Peter reared back and punched him square in the jaw.

"Peter! Stop it!"

Mattias was caught off guard for a split second and stumbled, then regained his footing in time to tackle Peter's torso as they both went flying into the door.

"Stop it, both of you!" I shouted, but it was no use. They couldn't hear me. I couldn't very well let them kill each other, my love and my best friend duking it out in my apartment. I was too short, too tiny to do much, so I did the first thing that came to mind. I went and grabbed the water pitcher out of my refrigerator and walked towards them with defiance in my eyes. I took the lid off and flung it onto them. In my mind, I watched them be so startled by cold water that they'd immediately stop fighting. I was wrong.

Most of it landed on Mattias, with his back still to me, and he stopped briefly and turned to me for one split second, long enough for Peter to land another hard blow to Mattias' beautiful face and knock him to the ground. Peter let him get back up before they started at each other again.

I was upset with Peter now. He was not my best friend anymore. He was a jerk who was beating up the man I loved. Why was he acting so childish, so foolish? He had ignored me and then proposed to me? He hadn't talked to me about anything regarding his feelings, let alone propose marriage out of the blue. Who does that?

These two tall handsome men were literally fighting over me, and I felt a rage rising in me that I had never known before. I was going to stop this absurdity, and since my first idea didn't work, I decided to try something else. I walked backward, past the couch, tucked my arms in, and put my head down. Then I ran with my right shoulder slightly outward, aimed straight for Peter. I hit him square in the chest, and he stumbled out onto the landing and fell.

I couldn't very well stop my little wadded-up body of inertia, and I tumbled down on top of him. My plan worked. I turned around to Mattias, who was looking down at us with an expression of equally mixed concern and amazement. He helped me up, and I told him to go inside and wait for me, which he did.

I turned to face Peter, still on the ground. I helped him to his feet and saw a look of betrayal and hurt on his beautiful face, now bruised and bloodied.

"That's it then," he said and left down the stairs. I couldn't tell if he was asking a question or making a statement with his tone. I wanted to follow him, to explain. I glanced inside at Mattias, who nodded at me to go. I ran down the stairs, half expecting to see Peter scooting away angrily. His scooter was not there, nor were any of its sounds. I looked first right and then left and saw him walking around the corner.

"Peter! Peter, please stop!" I was running as fast as I could, but I was far from prepared for this. I only had my socks and pajamas on, so I was freezing already, and it was hard to run on the concrete. I turned the corner and started running faster, yelling for him. It was not snowing outside anymore, but ice was in abundance on the sidewalk. I slipped on a patch and screamed in pain. Peter heard me and quickly came back, helping me up and brushing the snow off me. I was crying now. I had probably sprained my ankle. It started to swell, but I didn't care. He looked at me with a pain in his eyes so deep I didn't know what to do. He started walking away again.

"Peter, stop! It's not what you think!" I tried my best to limp after him. He stopped in his tracks and turned back around to face me. I said, "Mattias and I are the same. You and I are completely different!"

"So, you slept with him? He is in New York, in your apartment, and clearly overnight! I am in love with you, Cecelia! For f***'s sake, I just proposed to you! That was what you wanted!"

I was taken aback. I stumbled again and nearly fell backward from the shock. I had scarcely ever heard him utter a negative word of any sort, let alone a curse word so fiercely directed at me. Peter, though furious with me, held his hand out so that I could steady myself.

"Not from you," I whispered.

"What?" Peter looked confused and anguished.

I was more adamant through my tears and said again, "Not from you."

He stared at me, his ice-blue eyes looking wounded, betrayed. "It's not what you think, Peter. We didn't sleep together, and I didn't leave you for him."

His face turned to a serious expression, "I left you with him. Twice. Were you with him in Sweden?"

"No."

"Are you with him now?"

"Yes."

"Then it is what I think." He spun on his heels and stormed away. With frozen tears in my eyes, I defeatedly hobbled back around the corner and went painstakingly up the stairs to my apartment. Once inside, I did not immediately see Mattias. Further in, I heard him call my name from the balcony. I looked over, and he was standing outside in the cold air, leaning against the balcony. His back was to the street, his arms propped up on the rails with his long legs crossed in front of him. He had blood all over his shirt, a black eye, and a busted lip, but he still looked handsome.

The weather surrounded him in a foggy halo, and my heart was happy. I limped out to him, and he wrapped me in his arms. We held each other in the cold for a few minutes, calming each other down. "Come inside and let me patch you up," I said.

"Are you okay? Did he hurt you?" he asked sweetly concerned as he helped me over to the sink.

"No, I slipped on some ice and sprained my ankle is all. I'll be all right, but it might put a damper on our activities today. I was planning on us going to Central Park and take some photographs of the snow and scenery."

"Maybe tomorrow we'll do that. I think we have had enough fun for one day."

Mattias sat down on one of the barstools so I could take care of his face. "I think you'll probably have a black eye, but I can put a little bit of makeup on it if you're worried about your meetings." I pulled a bag of corn from the freezer for him to hold on it. I wiped the blood carefully from his lips and rubbed some medicated ointment on the bad places on his face and hands.

"No, I'll be fine. I'm not sure why Peter was so angry, but it felt good punching him, to be honest."

"He was angry because he thought we slept together."

"He was jealous? How long has it been since you were together?"

"He was beyond jealous. That's the thing. We didn't sleep together. I've only ever been with my husband. Peter asked, but I declined. When Peter heard you in here and saw you standing there in your pajamas and all your adorableness cooking for me, he assumed I had cheated on him with you more than once, and he lost it. Mattias, I can't be with someone that completely again unless I'm married to him. I just can't for my own sake...I need to know if that's something you're going to be okay with before this goes any further."

Mattias took my hands and held them in his. "Cecelia, I am hopelessly in love with you. Whatever you need, that is what I'll make happen." I kissed him hard, blood, medicine and all. He stood up, his tall Swedish frame shadowing mine, and then he swooped me up and carried me to the couch. "Now, let me take care of that ankle."

We didn't go to the park that weekend at all. We did exactly what I had imagined on the plane. We spent the whole time just curled up in each other's arms, away from the world. Sometimes kissing, sometimes watching whatever marathon was on television, and sometimes just watching the snow as it settled on the windowpanes.

Chapter 20

Monday came and went in the blink of an eye. Mattias was flying out Tuesday morning, and our time together was almost over. I missed him already, and I wished the distance from Sweden to New York wasn't so far.

Mattias had arranged for an exhibition six months from now, and I started panicking when I realized it might be that long before I saw him again. It had been nearly that long between our first and second times together, but that was different. I hadn't realized how much I had missed him and needed him in my life then.

Love is a funny thing. I had spent not even two full weeks with Mattias before he'd arrived in New York, but we were so immediately enlaced that we barely noticed how long we hadn't known each other. And here we were now, planning out the next phase of our life. The next morning, Mattias tried to make me feel better about his departure.

"Cecelia, don't worry like I know you already are. My leaving is far from goodbye. Don't stress yourself and overthink this. Please visit me in Norway in a month. I promise we won't go on anymore long road trips. I've found more inspiration in Norway lately, and I have a bigger studio there than in Gothenburg. You can come to help me select which paintings you think I should display. I haven't decided on an overall theme yet."

He grinned a grin I didn't quite recognize. "So, we can brainstorm." For a second, I felt he might be hiding something. He pulled me close to him and kissed me deeper, with more longing and passion than he'd done before. By now, we were old pros, becoming even more familiar with how the other one moved.

Tears were sliding down my cheeks again. "I miss you already." He laughed at me and rested his forehead on mine.

"Sweet Cecelia, your gray-green eyes are saddened, but my life started over when I met you."

I had tried calling Peter a few days later. I knew he was angry with both of us, but if I could explain things to him, maybe he'd understand. I was still a little confused by how angry he was since he hadn't told me he loved me the entire time we were together. Why did he decide to do it on my doorstep after weeks of not contacting me? And to propose on top of it, just because he thought that's what I wanted to hear?

Whenever I thought about it, I got mad again. Had Peter ever paid any attention to me at all, to think that's what I wanted? Still, I missed him. I missed my best friend. Maybe our conversations had never been as deep as I'd assumed. We had talked about God a little, he said he was a Christian, but we'd not talked about the subject of religion much more than that. How could I not have talked more about that? That's the basis of who I am.

Trying to recall any details while I was mad was difficult and only made my face flush. Whenever I'd mentioned Charlie, I'd mentioned God since they were so closely related to each other as far as my life had gone. Had he not felt as if he should try to compete with my dead husband? He had stayed in the shadows while my heart healed, believing that's what I'd needed. Except unknowingly, he had also pushed me into his brother's arms.

Peter had mentioned that it would be good for us to spend time together and had apparently concluded that Mattias needed to meet someone like him that could and would help him through his struggles. Peter hadn't realized that when Mattias and I met, we would bond so immediately, so interconnected to each other.

That had to be the only explanation for his sudden outburst of emotion. It hadn't been sudden for him at all. Peter had been my rock this whole time, that much I had realized, and he had been so incredibly patient with me. I couldn't imagine the pain he must feel now. Had he truly been in love with me the whole time?

His phone went straight to voicemail. I tried the next day again, with the same result. I hoped in time he would forgive us of the version he thought had happened. I missed his ice-blue eyes and the way he smiled at me, replaced now with deep sorrow when he looked at me.

This time, the month waiting to see Mattias was sheer agony for me. We talked on the phone nearly every day, but that just made it harder. I marked the days off on the calendar, and I checked my phone at least ten times a day, thinking maybe I had forgotten to mark the day, and it was already the next day. I kept thinking if I wished it hard enough, time would pass, and I would wake up the next day in Norway. I had booked my ticket to Oslo for the last week in February. Mattias had said that the airport wasn't too far from his cabin.

All I knew about Norway apart from our last beautiful trip there was what I had watched on TV when I was a little girl. The Winter Olympics were held in Lillehammer in 1994, and the only thing I could remember about the city was that there was lots of snow. More snow than I had seen there in October, and far more snow than I had ever been used to.

I bought extra socks, extra undergarments, and the biggest, heaviest coat I could find. I was going to look like the Michelin Man, but I'd be darned if I wasn't going to be prepared. I had not experienced Scandinavia in the dead of winter yet, but I was determined to win out against the elements.

When my plane flew in, the captain announced the typical arrival news, including the weather, which was twenty-five degrees Fahrenheit. Twenty-five. Degrees. Fahrenheit. I groaned and rolled my eyes as I pulled my scarf and beanie out of my suitcase and put my huge coat back on that I had been using as a pillow.

When Mattias saw me "pffting" in my large coat towards him with each step, he started laughing hysterically. "My love, are you warm enough? You prepared for the worst, but I promise I'll keep you indoors and comfortably warm."

He couldn't even wrap his arms around me this time. I pulled him to me and kissed him hard, with the same passion and intensity as the first time he had kissed me.

"This has been the longest month, and I hated it." He agreed and picked up my turtle suitcase.

His cabin was about a forty-five-minute drive outside of Oslo. Seeming to stretch on for ages, the road twisted and turned through the mountains, almost identical to our trip to Seven Sisters. It was only two in the afternoon, but it was dark and gloomy. Snowcapped mountains rose up around us on either side, and although it wasn't snowing when I had arrived, it started shortly after we started driving. It wasn't just regular American snow. This Scandinavian snow was heavy, chunky, and worthy of Santa himself.

We finally turned and started up one of the mountains, slowly because the roads were icier due to less traffic now. We passed an unusually thick patch of snow-covered trees and took a turn to go straight through them on a barely visible road. We might get snowed in.

I was only going to be here for a few days because that was all I could afford since this was going to be a regularly scheduled journey now. It didn't matter if we did got snowed in, that would be fine by me. Foot traffic at galleries generally slowed during freezing weather, which is what we were having in New York, but it didn't compare at all to the climate in Norway.

We finally arrived in a clearing and pulled up directly behind a gray building. The woods were just behind us now. In front of us was a plain, simple looking two-story gray house, and as we walked up a slight hill to get to the front door, Mattias said, "Let me show you the view."

We were almost to the front of the house, which was opposite of where we'd driven in from. As we walked up, I could see large windows leading out to a balcony overlooking a large, still lake with more jagged, snow-covered mountains directly behind it. The serene scene looked like a Bob Ross painting, and I marveled at the beauty.

I remembered the picture he had taken of the seagull on the rail, with these identical mountains behind it. He must've been doing all right for himself, better than I imagined, because if anyone in the States owned property with a view like this, it would've cost millions. "Mattias, can you afford this?" I asked curiously, as I was now worried for him and his financial security.

He laughed. "I rent it out to tourists during the spring, summer, and part of fall for quite a large amount, enough to pay for both of my homes. The lake and the view are big selling points, and I built a balcony on the main floor overlooking the landscape. Most of my renters are yearly, and most of them book the same weeks each year. It makes for a comfortable business arrangement. I live here in the winter to fix whatever I need to fix, and make sure it is as close to an upscale resort as I can make it."

"Oh, well that's smart, a good solution." He had told me before that he rented this one, but I hadn't remembered it until now.

Mattias opened a door on the bottom floor, and we walked inside. It was dark, but warmth surrounded my body instantly. He turned the light on, and in front of us was a staircase leading up to the main floor, while to our left was a closed door. "What's in there?" I asked. Mattias hesitated for a second. "My studio. I keep it locked so that the guests know it's off-limits."

"Can I see it now? What you've been working on these last few months?"

He hesitated again. "I'll show you tomorrow. Tonight, just relax and enjoy being here." There was something odd in his voice, but I didn't recognize it. I would let him keep whatever secret he was hiding until tomorrow, and take him up on is advice to relax.

When we got to the top floor, it was even warmer than the first floor. Where the stairway led up, we walked into an open floorplan. We were standing directly behind the living room and situated beside us to our left was a small kitchen with an island and barstools.

The layout reminded me a lot of his cabin in Sweden, only with dramatically different views. The glass door to the balcony was in the middle of the front, and on the other side was a small dining table and chairs. He had used earth tones for decorating. The walls were more of a gray-blue color, and the floors were a deep dark chocolate hardwood. A few paintings were hanging up that he had done of the surrounding landscape, and they were breathtaking. The paintings were so precise they looked like photographs themselves, better than even I could've taken. He was immeasurably talented.

A fireplace was located directly across from us, with a flat-screen TV hanging over it. Tying the room together was a few Norwegian trinkets, faux fur rugs, and a couch that was so large and inviting, even the most hardened and tough of the Scandinavian voyagers would rest their weary eyes for a while. I was impressed with how nice and well planned out it was. Not that his Sweden home wasn't lovely, but he had achieved five-star status with this one. Now I understood why he had regular customers.

To our right were three doors. The middle led to the bathroom, and on either side were two bedrooms, both large enough that either could've been the master. He set my suitcase down in the one on the right. I walked in and took my coat off, laying it across the bed. This bedroom was like his bedroom in Sweden. Several huge down comforters draped over the bed, and I noticed a chair in the corner holding two extra ones just in case.

Two large windows were on the right side, covered with large blackout curtains. I pulled one back to check out the view. I couldn't see the lake from here, but I could see the mountains looming over the cabin in all their rustic glory.

Mattias grilled herring for us that night on the stovetop, with fingerling potatoes and lingonberry jam. After dinner, he lit a fire in the fireplace. He had been uncharacteristically quiet throughout dinner, but we'd had a long day. He was probably just as tired as I was. We curled up in each other's arms on the couch to watch TV, with the extra down comforter over us, and that was the last thing I remembered.

I didn't wake up until the next morning. We were still on the couch, and Mattias was sound asleep with one arm wrapped around me. At some point, Mattias must've turned the television off because it was silent and peaceful. The fire was still flickering, but only barely. I had no idea what time it was, but it didn't matter. There were no clocks anywhere, and I had long decided I wasn't even going to pull my phone out on this trip. I was going to live in the moment from now on.

Mattias was lightly snoring in that adorable way he had done on our trip back from Abisko. I kissed him softly because I could. I sat up and tried to carefully roll out from under the down comforter so that he could continue to sleep, but I wasn't stealthy at all. I was tangled in the comforter and rolled onto the floor with a thud. I raised up and looked over the cushion at Mattias, but he didn't stir. At least I had been successful in that part.

I went into my bedroom to get my camera and coat, and silently crept out to the balcony. This foreign land was still freezing cold, far from the Savannah heat and humidity that still ran through my blood. I started shivering before I could even get my camera focused, but I kept going. I took shots of the lake, of the forest, of the vast landscape before me. I zoomed in on the mountains and took a few detailed shots.

I didn't hear Mattias walk up behind me, but I felt instantly warm as he wrapped his arms around my shoulders. "Good morning, love." I turned around to kiss him but decided against it. Instead, I buried my freezing face into his chest. He laughed a deep, hearty laugh. "How about we go inside for breakfast?"

He didn't make me try any more blood sausage this time, thank goodness. Instead, he fixed his usual morning specialty of bacon and eggs.

"What are your initial ideas for your exhibition? You have so much material to work with just from this location. Are you thinking of using your landscapes? I'd like to see the rest of them."

He laughed a little, seeming a bit nervous as he avoided my question. "We can talk about that later on."

I was curious now as to why he kept acting evasive, so I pushed a little more.

"Can we go down and look at them after breakfast?"

He looked at me with his deep blue eyes, a light shining in them that I remembered from when he'd first kissed me. He took a deep breath as if something was weighing on him.

"Yes, Cecelia, I will show you what I have been working on after we're done eating."

I looked at him strangely. I wasn't sure what to make of the expression that was now on his face. Was he tired? Was he mad at me? Was he having second thoughts about us? I tried not to let myself overthink and jump to the worst conclusions. I was a pro at that.

After breakfast, he excused himself for a minute to go to his bedroom. When he came back, he still had that same expression on his face, and now I was getting worried. "Mattias, is everything okay? You're worrying me. I can't read your face."

"Yes, Cecelia, all is fine. I want you to know that no matter what you think downstairs, I love you. I am desperately in love with you."

"Oh man, are you a serial killer? Are there dead bodies down there, and you don't want me to freak out? That would be my luck." Again, I really needed stop watching true crime documentaries.

He laughed, his face relaxing, "Okay, maybe not quite that bad." We walked downstairs in silence. I was so nervous now, not knowing what to expect or what to feel, and my hands became clammy. Had I been wrong about him? Did he paint horrible imagery like crime scene murders and weird things like that? That must be it. He had not shown me his portfolio when he came to New York, and I had not even asked if I could see it. I was so happy just to have him in front of me. Should I have asked more questions?

He unlocked the door, and we walked inside to darkness. A rush of cold hit me, and I instantly decided that there must be frozen bodies down here. Logic kicked in, and I realized that heat rises, and he probably had not lit the fireplace down here in a few days at least. I could tell we were in a large room and that several easels were set up with canvases, with still more canvases leaning against the walls. He turned the lights on, which were so bright I had to close my eyes for a few seconds.

"Cecelia, I want to tell you how much you have changed me. I did not want change, I did not expect it, but I was in love with you the moment I saw you."

As tender as his words were, I wasn't fully listening to him. My eyes were adjusting and trying to figure out the paintings before me, and I got lost in my surroundings. My eyes bounced around the room at all the canvases, all the colors and scenes and faces before me grabbed my attention. The room was divided into two sections—one side held landscapes, and the other side held portraits and sketches, studies of random people. The faces were the focus of most of these paintings, and he had paid close attention to light and shadow.

I saw a few that reminded me of Caravaggio, the Italian painter who was known for his stark contrast of light and dark. I smiled, remembering fondly my years studying at SCAD.

I began to get a feeling of immense appreciation for Mattias' talents. He truly was a jack of all trades, mastering many different mediums and genres.

I looked now at the canvases immediately in front of me, which were much different. Large paintings, most of them at least four by six feet, spread out before me over the entire room. The surfaces of every canvas on this side of the room were covered, and every inch of the walls on this side had canvases leaning up against them. These paintings were not like his other studies but were all entirely different. They were brighter, full of color, and they all focused on specific parts of the subject—an outline of a face, a nose, the angle shadows and light across two people, which all looked vaguely familiar. They reminded me of the Impressionist masters, but I could not place the subjects immediately. These people as he painted them, they were beautiful, angelic even. He had clearly been inspired by something different when painting these.

He continued talking behind me, and I tried to explore and listen at the same time.

"I didn't think I could heal, that I could love anybody again. This is coming out so awful. What I mean to say is you changed my perspective and my inspiration."

I walked to another one, which was of a woman's eyes. They were gray-green. I inhaled quickly as I noticed a photograph clipped to the top of the canvas. I looked around, noticing that all of the easels had a photo clipped to them, focusing specifically on the subject. I did know these people. They were us. These were the photos I had taken of Mattias and me at Abisko the first time we met. I had forgotten I had even mailed them to him.

He had enlarged portions of them, focused on certain features, and then reimagined them from his mind. They were breathtaking, so detailed and vibrant they must've included all spectrums of the color wheel.

I was so touched and was moved to tears. "Mattias, you painted us! They're amazing! I can't believe you did all these!" I wheeled around to face him, the first time since we had walked down here. He was down on one knee, holding a small box. "Cecelia, please let me say this before you say anything. I know that this is incredibly, so incredibly soon, but I also knew I wanted to marry you from the first moment I met you. And as I got to know you over the next few days, I knew we would be here." His voice was shaking with emotion as he continued.

"You have inspired every corner of my mind. You have changed me, Cecelia. Completely, internally, externally, spiritually. My thoughts are different, my hopes are different, my beliefs are different. I did not think any of that was possible, but you made it so. God is very much alive and brought you to me, of that I am certain. Through you, He has changed me, and I resemble nothing of my old self. I want a future with you, Cecelia. You are my life and my love, and I am fully devoted to you."

"Mattias, I—"

He put his hand up. "Please let me say this. I'm terrified that you think this is too soon, and I'm afraid it will all come out wrong. I have three questions to ask you."

"Okay." I was smiling from ear to ear but was trying to be serious too. I was going to let him finish, he was so cute and scared, but I already knew what my answer was to one of them at least.

"It is important for you to understand I am in no way pressuring you to say anything right now. I had planned on doing this during this week, when you would be here, but upon further reflection, it is very soon into our relationship. I'd like for you to at least think about these questions. Take your time. Take months if you need to. Whatever you need."

I nodded, giggling now because he was nervously shaking. I wanted to kiss him right then, but I didn't want to interrupt the concentration he was working so hard to maintain.

"Okay, here goes. Question one. I have been thinking a lot in the last month, and I was wondering if it would be all right with you if I moved to New York?"

I opened my mouth to speak, instantly gratified that he had asked me this. I didn't think I could go another long month, or longer, without seeing him. He didn't give me a chance to answer.

"Question two." He opened the box, and inside was the most beautiful emerald ring. I knew this ring. I had noticed it the night I'd met his parents at the opera. His mom had been wearing it as her wedding ring, and I remembered thinking the antique looked radiant and well taken care of. It was at least several carats, and it had a halo of diamonds around it that continued onto the silver band on either side. It must've been a family heirloom.

"Cecelia Sweeting, will you do me the enormous honor of being my wife?"

I couldn't stand it anymore. I flung myself at him and kissed him, kissed his face, kissed his neck. "Yes! Yes, to both! I don't have to think about it, Mattias. I've been in love with you the whole time!" I'd almost forgotten the final question, and so had he. He helped me up to my feet, and I said, "Wait, what is the third question?" He placed the ring on my finger. "I was wondering if you might baptize me in the lake sometime in these next few days?"

I immediately thought of Charlie, how we had started, and how

God had brought my life full circle. "It would be my absolute honor."

Chapter 21

Mattias and I both changed into white clothes for his baptism, symbolic of God and the purity between us. Since the lake was freezing, we took extra comforters to wrap up in afterward. The weather was different now from what it had been, even as early as that morning when I was taking pictures. It was not gloomy and foggy anymore but had changed as quickly as the weather in Savannah.

It was still cold, but the wind wasn't blowing at all. The snow had also stopped since yesterday, and we could see the sun spilling over the tops of the mountains onto us and the lake. The air was smooth and calm, and as we walked towards the water, I could feel Mattias' hand tighten around my own.

"This is the most beautiful thing you could ever do with your life," I said to encourage him. We reached the lake's edge. "Let me explain what I'm going to do before we walk in. I'm going to say a few sentences, and you'll repeat them back to me. Then, I'll lean you back, fully into the water for a few seconds."

He nodded, and we both let out a small shriek as we stepped into the freezing water.

It was extremely uncomfortable. I felt my skin started shrinking and shriveling inward from the cold, trying to escape it. Dark water had always been one of my biggest fears. I hated not knowing, not seeing what was around me, and the feeling of being helpless in an unfriendly element.

My body hesitated to keep walking, but I pushed my fear away. This was not about me. I had no logical reason to be afraid, we were probably safe from sharks since they most likely didn't live in Norwegian lakes. When we were waist-deep, we stopped. I stood sideways beside Mattias, facing him, and I put one hand on his back, the other holding his hand. I could see our breath clearly as we stood there, but the sun was shining down on us, and I could also feel a little bit of warmth from it.

"Do you accept Jesus as your Lord and Savior?"

"I do."

"Do you believe that He died and rose again, the Son of God?"

"I believe."

I spoke, and Mattias repeated. "I, Mattias Levander, believe fully in my heart and soul that Jesus Christ is the Son of the living God." My heart caught even more emblazoned fire for him right then. This must've been how Charlie had felt so many years ago, and it was one of the most beautiful moments I had ever experienced. "I baptize you in the name of the Father, the Son, and the Holy Ghost. May they keep you and bless your eternal life."

I crossed his arms on his chest, put one hand on the back of his head, and leaned him backward into the glassy water. By now, the cold was not as cold for me. My skin had adjusted and become numb. As the water rushed over him, I felt the warmth of the sun on us fully now. "God, thank you for this man," I prayed aloud. I raised him as soon as he was submerged, and though he was shivering, he looked lighter. There's something in the water, I reminded myself. I kissed his precious face, and we raced back up to the comforters awaiting us.

We ran inside to our separate bedrooms and immediately changed into dry, heavier clothes. I finished first, and I went and started up the fireplace as high as I could get it to go. Mattias walked up behind me, wrapped his arms around my waist, and kissed my neck.

I turned around, facing him. "How do you feel?"

"Changed. I feel changed. I know I was in the water for a split second, but when I was there, it was like time slowed down. It was a strange, surreal feeling. I saw everything. I saw where I had been, the man I used to be, and where I am now. As you started to raise me, I felt hands all over me, demons and doubts and fears, trying to pull me back down into the dark. But I refused them all." He was crying, and I was crying.

"I'm so proud of you," I said as I kissed him. There was something about this kiss that felt different, more solid and certain than before. We rolled ourselves up into the comforter and sat down on the couch, trying to regain our heat. We stayed there for a long time talking about numerous subjects, from other native foods Mattias could have me try, to what we would do about our New York situation. We couldn't plan our New York life out very well without first giving our wedding a date. They went hand in hand as to how we were going to approach the rest.

We decided we wanted it to be sooner rather than later. The distance between our countries was too great and the monetary cost too high to keep going back and forth. We were both doing well for ourselves, but if we made too many more trips too close together, we would start to drain our resources.

We decided to set the date for the end of April, nearly eight weeks away and much warmer. It was incredibly soon for most people, but to us, it felt far off in the distance. We decided that was the longest possible amount of time we could go without seeing each other again, and the shortest amount possible to be acceptable in social circles.

We had just a few people on our guest list. On Mattias' side, he wanted just his family: his parents, younger brother, and Peter if he would come. I wanted Brad and Shelly, Roger, and my parents. I sent Roger a quick text, asking if he would be available on that date for a job. I told him I had someone who needed an impromptu wedding on a small budget, but I didn't give him any further details. I wanted to break the news to everyone myself. A text message from Roger would travel like wildfire through Savannah.

I knew planning it out would be right up Roger's alley, and not having to worry about the details didn't stress me at all. Details were meant to be shown in pictures, not in stress lines on your face. As far as Mattias and I were concerned, we could just get married under a nice tree. Who a person marries matters far more than how a person marries ever will. Mattias suggested we go to McDonald's for the reception, and we laughed and laughed.

"When did you know you were going to marry me?" I knew he had told me this already, but I couldn't help wanting to hear it again. "Instantly, when I first saw you. Then that second night, in the kitchen, was when I knew for sure. The way you spoke, it was like you were inside my head already. No one had ever understood me like that before, and I knew I must keep you in whatever way I could. I knew you weren't serious with my brother before I had even asked. I could feel it in the way you smiled at me. When did you fall in love with me?"

I thought about it. Had there been a specific moment? Or had it just been his whole aura and presence that had drawn me in?

"I think immediately, but I also think there wasn't a specific moment, and then there were a lot of moments. When I first heard your music, that had been in my dream, I felt the strongest sense of déjà vu I had ever felt in my life. The night at the rave, dancing so close to you and not feeling ashamed or awkward, we were like two puzzle pieces that fit perfectly together. Any moment I was with you could've been 'the moment.' I didn't know it, or I didn't admit it to myself. When Peter ditched me the second time, I was thrilled to be spending more time with you, and I instantly knew when you picked me up at the airport that I wanted you for the rest of my life."

"Ah, that was why you started crying?"

"Yes, but I was so afraid of telling you. I didn't want to hurt Peter, and I didn't want you to think less of me. I started thinking of scenarios where everything went wrong, and I just started crying."

"Sweet Cecelia, nothing will go wrong now." He was silent for a second. "Oh. I forgot to tell you one thing. My parents are coming up tomorrow to see you. My mom knew I was going to propose, and they want to welcome you into the family officially. Surprise!"

His parents arrived the next day, around lunchtime. They were still the same tall, radiantly beautiful people I remembered, only now dressed more warmly. I remembered his mom had an impeccable style, and she did not disappoint now. She looked as if she had just walked out of a ski resort in Aspen, dressed in a light purple snowsuit with her hair swept up in a ponytail.

His dad was no different, although possibly in a different time altogether. He wore a well-tailored dark gray three-piece suit, with a light purple shirt and pocket square to match his wife, underneath a large wool trench coat. I couldn't help but notice how much he reminded me of Peter the first few times I'd met him, right down to the golden hair, only an older version.

"Dad always goes for formal," Mattias whispered in my ear as they were walking up. "I think that's where Peter gets it from."

"Hello, dear!" His mom swiped me up into her arms for a giant hug. His dad held out his hand, and we shook.

"Hello sir, ma'am."

"Oh, nonsense. I think it's time for less formal introductions. You may call us Einar and Astrid." She grabbed my left hand, her eyes sparkling. "I see all went well, my future daughter! You know, this ring has a story, I must tell you, but first I am famished!"

We went inside. Mattias had roasted a chicken and some vegetables just a short while before, and I had already set the table. They took their coats off and settled in, while Mattias served our plates.

"We won't stay for very long. We don't want to intrude, but we just had to come to welcome you to the family!" Astrid said. She took a small box out of the pocket of her jacket coat and laid it in front of me.

"Now, dear Cecelia, I must tell you the story before I get too excited and forget. That emerald ring, now yours, has been in our family for six generations. Tradition goes that in each generation the first man to ask for it from his mother gets to propose to his intended with it."

I was overcome with emotion and gratitude at hearing about and now being a part of such a legacy. "It's insanely beautiful and well taken care of."

"Yes, it is a great family treasure that six generations of Levander women have protected and cherished. Upon hearing Peter talk about you, I thought he might be the one to ask for it. I don't know what all has happened between you and my oldest son, but I immediately knew that Mattias had fallen in love with you as soon as he told me about you. He had not spoken so passionately about anyone or anything in a long while. After meeting you at the opera, I knew in an instant that Mattias would be the one to ask for the ring. And he did ask me for it, the day after you left." I looked over at Mattias, who was grinning and slightly blushing. He'd had it for several months! What an adorable little secret he'd been keeping from me.

"I think Peter hates me now," I said.

"Peter is hard to figure out. He's just like his father." She reached over and held Einar's hand before continuing. "He's been hard to read ever since he was a baby, and that is not your fault. He's stoic and appears to lack emotion, which is also not your fault. He will come around. He just needs time to process."

"Aren't you angry with me? For breaking his heart?" I asked, confused by her kindness.

"No, dear. You cannot fight love, no matter the situation," Astrid said warmly.

She picked up the small box. "Also, a tradition amongst Levander women is this. Since we don't get to keep the emerald indefinitely, the mother must buy something for her daughter that she can keep and call her own. Einar's mother gave me this necklace." She reached for the chain around her neck, revealing the pendant I had seen at the opera. It was an emerald about the size of a nickel, surrounded in a halo of white diamonds I now could see more clearly. If I hadn't known the ring and pendant weren't a set, I wouldn't have been able to tell.

"Oh my, that's beautiful."

"Yes, and one-hundred percent real. As are these," Astrid said as she opened the box. Inside was a set of emerald stud earrings, again so radiant, and matched the ring so perfectly that I couldn't tell they weren't part of a set.

"Oh, Astrid, they're gorgeous! I don't know what to say!" I immediately picked the box up to look to take a closer look. They were small enough that I would be able to wear them daily without being overly flashy, but large enough to be grand and elegant in their own right. Perfection. "You'll have many sons. I am sure of it. Remember to keep these traditions going."

The four of us sat at the table for several hours, talking and laughing and telling stories. We told them of our plans, and they were delighted. They didn't think it was too soon at all. They had been married six months after they'd started dating, and that had worked out well for them. Astrid booked airline tickets while we were talking, and Mattias and I looked at each other and smiled. We had told our first family members now, and it was officially happening in eight weeks! They left in the late afternoon to begin their journey back to Gothenburg.

Chapter 22

Leaving Mattias this time was bittersweet. It was easier, knowing the next time I'd see him, he would soon be my husband. It was harder because now I had to go eight weeks without seeing him, knowing he would soon be my husband. He had decided he wanted Peter to be his best man if he would, and we both promised to reach out to him. I didn't know how Peter would respond. I hadn't talked to or seen him at all since he and Mattias had fought. I didn't feel it would be fair of us to not try and include him, even if he didn't want to be there.

When I got back to New York, I called my parents first and told them the news. "April 28th, Mama! You and Daddy need to be in New York on April 28th because I'm getting married!" Mama was stunned at first, and then so excited I had to hold the phone away from my ear because she was shrieking so loud.

"Now is this that handsome curator fella you told me about?"

"No, it's actually his brother." Awkward silence. I went into the whole story, realizing as I'd told it I would have to repeat it to Shelly too. I had kept Mattias all to myself, my secret love. When I got to the baptism part, Mama said, "Oh honey, Charlie was watching out for you this whole time."

"Yes, Mama, he was."

Roger had texted me back, saying he was available, and he had texted several more times asking for more detail. I knew I needed to call him, but I decided to call Shelly first. The phone rang.

"C! Long time no talk! How in the world are ya?"

"I'm doing well, Shelly! Hey, listen, I'm calling to ask you a favor. Do you think you could be my maid of honor on April 28th?" The same thing happened again as with my mom, loud shrieking and me holding the phone away from my face. "Cecelia! Peter proposed?"

"Well, technically yes. But I'm not marrying him." The same awkward silence, as I went into the whole story again. When I had finished, I awaited Shelly's response.

"Hold on and let me get this straight. What you're telling me is that while you were casually dating Handsome Number One, secretly you were in love with Handsome Number Two. Who happens to be so spiritually identical to you that you immediately were drawn to him from the get-go. As soon as you realized he was the one you were in love with, you dumped Handsome Number One, and three months later, you're marrying Handsome Number Two. Is that what I'm hearing?"

I giggled at her Southern accent. She sounded like home, and I missed her bluntness. "Yes, so will you be my maid of honor?"

"Absa-flippin-lutely! You know, not for nothin', but this is all God's and my doing anyway. He told me I had to push you, and if I hadn't pushed you to move to New York, you never would've gotten involved in this love triangle. You're welcome for setting you up with your new husband."

"Yes, I think you're right. What color dress would you like to wear? And start thinking about your shoes because it should be warm enough to wear something open-toed if you want!"

After hanging up with Shelly, I called Roger immediately. I went through the whole story again, for the third time now. He was full of logical planning questions.

"Roger, honestly, plan whatever you want. I'm fine with it being a surprise. Just don't go over budget. There's only going to be maybe twelve people there. I'll give you everybody's phone numbers, and I'll hire you to coordinate it in whatever way you want."

"What colors do you want?"

"A spring color theme. A fresh new start."

I had a newfound confidence that I hadn't known before. I was more certain of myself, more fearless, and feistier. I don't know how to describe it, but I wasn't quiet, passive Cecelia anymore. I had found my voice. It wasn't because of Mattias, but also it was. I certainly didn't need a man to complete me, but I did feel complete. I was blessed with a second soulmate, and I felt whole again. God came through in a big, huge way, and I was on fire!

I gave it a month and then tried calling Peter again. I wanted to make sure he had the option of attending or not. It was important to both of us. Straight to voicemail. The next time I talked to Mattias, he had not been able to reach Peter either. I was highly irritated, and I decided I would counter his behavior with similar childish behavior. If he was going to shut me out, then I was going to face him head-on, as I had when we'd first met. That had worked out well then, throwing him off his serious, professional game. It was going to work now.

I made a pan of tiramisu, his absolute favorite dessert, to bring to him. That might win him over or at least get me in the door. The Southern spirit in my soul took over. I pulled my ponytail through a baseball cap and put on my blue jeans, a T-shirt, and my hoop earrings before marching the two blocks to his apartment. Fighting clothes. The closer I got with each step, the fiercer and more determined I felt. Nobody messes with a Southern girl when she's wearing hoop earrings. That's the international sign that you better shape up or ship out.

His scooter was outside, I was in luck. I buzzed the front door, but he did not answer and did not buzz me in. Just then, Tara—Peter's neighbor whom I had to put in her place the first time I went dancing with Peter—opened the door. We stared each other down as she stood in the doorway. I had my hoops in, and I was ready to take her on if need be.

I spoke first. "Hello."

"Hello." We squinted our eyes as we each sized up our opponent.

"Is that for Peter? I haven't seen you around here lately, or at dance class."

"We've both been busy traveling. I'd appreciate it if you could hold the door open for me, Tara," I said in my nicest, passive aggressive Southern drawl.

"Of course, Cecelia. That's a beautiful ring you have on." She wrinkled her nose at my emerald as she stepped to the side for me to pass.

"Oh yes, didn't Peter tell you? I'm going to be a Levander soon!" She gave me a death stare, turned, and slammed the door behind me. I just grinned to myself.

I marched up the two flights of stairs and beat on his apartment door. No answer. I pounded harder. "Peter Levander, you open this door this instant!" My Southern drawl started coming back out. No answer. "Peter! I'm serious! I have tiramisu, and I'm not leaving!" I heard a shuffle and finally he opened the door slowly, in pajama pants and a plain black T-shirt. He looked even paler than usual.

"Cecelia, what do you want?"

"You look like death warmed over. Are you all right?"

I pushed my way past him and into his apartment with my tiramisu. A sea of tissues and blankets were all over the couch.

"No, I have the flu or some ailment. I've done nothing but sleep for the last few days."

"Well, you're going to talk to me whether you like it or not, so you just better get over it. Do you have any chicken broth?"

"No. What are you doing here?" He stopped fighting my presence long enough to glance down at my hand. His face fell. "You have Mom's ring," he said matter-of-factly.

"Yes, Peter, that's why I'm here. I wanted to talk to you, but I see you're not in the right frame of health to listen. I'm going to go down to the store and buy you some groceries. When I come back, you'd better let me in, or so help me I will bust this door down." I put the tiramisu in the refrigerator and left.

I came back with a few boxes of chicken broth, some orange juice, energy drinks, celery, carrots, chicken, corn, and a few other odds and ends. Peter didn't keep many groceries in his apartment other than what he was immediately cooking, so I bought whatever I could think of that I might need, including a cheap stockpot. I put all the stew ingredients into the pot, turned it on medium-high, and sat down with Peter.

"You look different, Cecelia. More confident."

"Thank you. I am. Peter, I'll get straight to the point. Mattias and I are getting married in a month, and we want you to be the best man. I love you, and I would like it if you could forgive me and be my best friend again. I need you in my life, and Mattias needs you in his. You're his big brother. He and I, we're the same. We've had so much happen between us before we were even engaged, I couldn't even begin to make you understand all that we share. I didn't mean to hurt you. I wouldn't ever hurt you on purpose."

He blew his nose, which was bright red against his ghostly face.

"Peter, I didn't sleep with Mattias. Not the times in Sweden and Norway, New York or even after he proposed. He was in town, staying in my guest room when you saw him. That's why he was in my apartment when you walked in; I cross my heart. I need you to understand that part, at least."

He nodded, trying to listen while trying to stay awake. "I want you in our wedding, and Mattias wants you there. Your parents and your brother are coming, so are my parents and my best friends from Savannah. You are an integral part of our life, so please say you'll be the best man."

"Cecelia, I will forgive you both in time, but not right now. I cannot be there. I will not watch you marry my brother. I am sorry for not being there for you more when you needed me. Maybe things would be different if I had not left you alone with him. Do you think that would have changed anything? I keep playing it out, where was I wrong?"

I hugged him. "Peter, you weren't wrong. I don't think we were ever meant to be in love."

He hugged me back. "Cecelia, please just go."

"No, not until I see you eat some soup."

Chapter 23

Shelly had flown out the next weekend after I called her so that we could go shopping for dresses. She found a light olive-green dress that complemented her hair and skin tone nicely. It was sleeveless chiffon, so it moved and swayed freely, and the skirt came down to just below her knees.

I found the perfect dress in a vintage shop, just like I had found my first wedding dress years ago. This one was covered in ivory lace with long lace sleeves that came up and buttoned behind the neck. It was open across the shoulders, with buttons running from the lower back all the way to the bottom on the train. It was floor-length, very fitted, and straight down with a train of about a foot. Very simple, but the lace made it elegant and chic. I couldn't help but think Astrid would probably love it too.

The rest of the weeks came and went quickly and slowly. I rearranged my apartment and cleaned out a bunch of old clothes and random things to make room for Mattias. I took the bed down in the guest bedroom and propped the mattress and frame up against the wall. Mattias could use it as his studio. It only had one tiny window and felt drab, dreary, and non-inspirational. It was sizeable enough for a start, but it was a temporary solution that we would have to work out once he was here.

He had started shipping a few smaller boxes of his things so that when he arrived, he wouldn't have to go back for quite a while. Most of the boxes contained books and clothes, and I unpacked them for him so that I could smell his scent. I was so thankful to God for all that I had in my life. Even though I had lost so much, God had matched it back tenfold in my heart.

Roger had rounded up some of his Broadway friends to help him and had assured me that my wedding would be the most extravagant budget wedding of the century. He had a few surprises up his sleeve, as did Shelly, but they would not tell me what they were. He wouldn't even tell me the exact location until the morning of the nuptials.

Everyone flew in the day before, including my parents, Mattias' parents, Brad and Shelly, and Mattias. Roger was the biggest help. He should have been an event planner with the detail he put into the whole thing. He rented a Mercedes Sprinter, the most luxurious van he could find, and picked our group up at the airport and shuttled them to a hotel directly beside Central Park. He had blocked several rooms on one floor so we could all be together, and he arranged for a rehearsal dinner a short walk away.

"Surprise number one, I got ordained, and I will be performin' yer ceremony!" Roger whispered in my ear as we walked into the restaurant. He had picked a five-star steakhouse directly beside

Central Park, and as the group entered and took their seats, he stood up with an empty water glass.

"Attention, attention! I'd like to tank ye all fer comin'! I have a few announcements to make! First, before ye check out and go home, make sure the desk clerk knows ye are part of the Sweeting/Levander party, and ye will get a ten percent discount fer bookin' bulk!"

Thunderous applause roared from our small table. New York was not cheap. "Second of all, Cecelia and Mattias don't even know this, I am now going to announce the weddin' location! As ye all might've guessed, it'll be held in Central Park! What ye don't rightly know is that it'll be at Bet'esda Terrace! Surprise number two!"

Our small crowd cheered in excitement. People either already knew Bethesda Terrace or started googling it on their phones immediately. It had been featured in countless movies and television shows, so they all got excited at recognizing it as soon as it popped up on their phones.

"The weddin' will be held at tree!"

Shelly stood up and said, "That's three o'clock in American English, everybody."

We all laughed, including Roger, who said, "Bet'esda can only be booked for the afternoon because night crowds are a wee bit wild and crowded, so the reception might be intruded on by local passersby. Don't be alarmed. Tey're friendly!"

Mattias leaned over and kissed my cheek. We had not had a moment to ourselves since he'd arrived, and we wouldn't until after the wedding. "I missed you, love."

I kissed his sweet lips. "Tomorrow I'll be your wife." The rest of the night was kind of a blur for me. I was so excited and happy to be marrying Mattias tomorrow, I could think of little else. I had ordered grilled chicken for dinner, but I barely ate any of it. My adrenaline was keeping me full.

That night the adrenaline kept me awake too. As I tossed and turned, I just kept thinking how Mattias would be mine tomorrow, and how great it was that I had hired Roger to take care of all the details. If I hadn't, I would've been a nervous wreck by now.

I woke up to beating on my door. I rolled out of bed and looked at the clock, which showed 9:00 a.m. Six more hours before I would be married to Mattias. It might as well have been a century; that's how it felt. I opened the door as Shelly, my mom, and Astrid came rushing in with makeup bags and hair rollers and all sorts of shenanigans up their sleeves. They were all wearing matching 'Team Bride' bedazzled tank tops, sweat pants and flip flops.

"Cecelia! Get in the shower! I have to do your hair!" Mama barked as I noticed Shelly going through the closet and pulling out my dress. She strung it up on the back of the closet door and pulled out a travel steamer so she could get all wrinkles out, visible to the naked eye or not. "Your 'something old' needs to look loved or it doesn't count!" Shelly fussed at me. I laughed and went into the bathroom to take a quick shower.

When I came out, Shelly was done steaming my dress and had started fashioning a bouquet out of buckets of flowers she had acquired from who knows where. Multiple shades of colors of peonies and lilies were placed in five-gallon tubs all over the place, and the room smelled fabulous now.

Astrid had converted the vanity into a make-up studio in no time at all, and I had never seen so many colors of shadows, powders and foundations. Tools and brushes were scattered all over. I had no idea what most of them were even for.

Mama had a few curlers left that weren't already rolled up around her head. They were heating up, the old-fashioned ones in the heat box, and beside them lay about a thousand bobby pins and at least two gallons of hair spray. If you didn't have big hair in the South, you were nothing. After she had finished styling my hair, Mama stuck white daisies in it for good measure, very vintage chic. I stood up on a chair so Mama could double check all of the buttons just as someone knocked on the door.

I turned around to see who it was just as Shelly reached the door. I saw her jaw fall open in disbelief as she stood aside. In walked Peter, more handsome than I had ever seen him. He was wearing a dark gray tuxedo to match Mattias, and his hair was slicked back as was his custom. In my peripherals, I saw Mama's eyes widen as Astrid walked over and kissed his cheek. Shelly looked from him to me in disbelief, now realizing that this extremely handsome man was the first brother I had been dating. Mama looked up at me, also realizing who he was.

Peter glanced around the room until me met my gaze.

"Can ya'll give us a minute?" I asked.

"Of course, dear," Astrid said as Mama and Shelly walked out silently, their eyes still wide.

Peter walked over to me and held out his hand so I could step off the chair without falling over.

"You're here." I looked up at him, smiling.

"I'm here," Peter said calmly, softly. He leaned over and kissed my cheek. "I realized that despite my feelings, I didn't want this to tarnish our relationship, or my relationship with Mattias. You're beautiful." He held my hands in his as he raised them up to his lips.

"I'm glad you came."

Just then, the door flew open as Mama, Astrid and Shelly rushed back in. I hadn't been keeping up with the time. Shelly ran over and grabbed a yellow peony, pinned it to Peter's tuxedo and shoved him out the door.

"We need to start walking at two! Roger gave us strict instructions on where we're supposed to go so that Mattias doesn't see you. You cannot leave this room any earlier than two, or you might run into him!" Mama was beside herself. I knew our wedding was as important to them as it was to us, and it made me smile.

"Your 'something blue' is the ribbon I'm tying around your bouquet," I heard Shelly say from the corner as she furiously wrapped a light blue ribbon up the base of the flowers. "And your something old is your vintage dress," She repeated, pleased that she could see no wrinkles after her aggressive steaming.

"My 'something new' is my shoes. I spent a fortune on them." And I had. I had found the prettiest, most perfect pair of white Christian Louboutin strappy heels imaginable. I wasn't one to spend quite that much on shoes, but today wasn't just any day.

"Your 'something borrowed' is this, dear." Astrid took off her emerald necklace and placed it around my neck.

"Oh! Are you sure?"

"Of course, I am sure. It will look like a full set!"

I had planned on wearing my emerald earrings, so this was the best 'borrowed' I could've had. They had all brought their dresses over as well and rapidly took turns changing and doing each other's makeup. Finally, it was time to go. My last walk as a single woman, again.

Roger had instructed us to wait behind the fountain, my back to it so that I could not see the terrace, and Mattias could not see me. A few people were out at this hour, but not as many as I had imagined. It was a beautiful, bright sunny day. The weather was warm but not hot, and a gentle breeze was blowing through. It was silent too, except for the fountain behind me and the birds chirping in the trees not far off.

Mama and Astrid went to their seats. Walking up, I had seen only a few chairs were on either side of the middle arch of the terrace, but I had not looked closer for fear of being seen. Daddy, Shelly, and I were left to wait at the fountain, and a few minutes before 3:00, I heard a violin start playing.

"Okay," said Shelly. "I'm going to start walking slowly. Count to five and then start walking around the other side of the fountain." Off she went.

As soon as the violinist saw me, the "Bridal March" began. Our little group was already standing, and I could see Mattias now. He was in a dark gray tuxedo, and he looked delicious. For a second I believed I was probably in a dream, and then I remembered this was real. I couldn't take my eyes off him. He was smiling and glowing radiantly at me. I prayed silently, *God, this is the gentlest, kindest, most perfect man that You could have possibly sent me. Thank You for thinking so much of me to send me this gift.*

Roger pronounced us husband and wife a few minutes after 3:00. I threw my bouquet out into our tiny crowd and jumped into Mattias' awaiting arms. He kissed me hard, and I kissed him back harder. Our kiss lasted for longer than it should have, but I didn't care. I was his, and he was mine, and as he went to kiss me again, I whispered, "Hello, husband."

Our tiny crowd was still cheering us on as I looked out towards the fountain. Another larger crowd of strangers had gathered and they were also cheering for us. Roger pulled up a chair and stood on it. "Attention guests of the weddin' and citizens of New York! Food carts are on the way! They are donating food to the first one hundred people and donating their time for a marketin' opportunity! So please stay tuned for the reception and post plenty of pictures!"

The promise of free food drew even more cheers from the larger crowd. Roger turned to me and said, "Surprise number tree, I advertised on me blog and got quite a lot o' feedback. In exchange for a full-length story about their business on me blog, two food carts are comin' to supply hot dogs and pretzels! Aye, that's authentic New York food!" Mattias and I laughed and agreed that was perfect for our wedding.

Shelly grabbed our arms. "Okay, now it's my turn! Surprise number four! Since you obviously can't photograph your wedding, that's the first of our two gifts to you! But we've got to go now while the light is perfect!"

We raced over to the fountain, up onto the terrace, under the terrace, taking multiple pictures as quickly as we could before the sun went down and before too many people crowded around us. I heard both Mattias' and my stomach growling. "We'll take more afterward, but I just had to get some with great lighting!"

By the time we were done with the initial photos, the food carts had arrived. Shelly said, "I'm going to go take pictures of the family. Ya'll go up under the terrace. Roger has a small buffet waiting for just the wedding party." Sure enough, just out of sight from the crowds was a small eight-foot table set up with hot dogs, sodas, pretzels, and condiments. We were both starving by then, as neither of us had eaten all day. I ate two hot dogs, and Mattias unashamedly ate four.

Roger then made another announcement, that it was time for us to cut the "cake." Brad brought over a giant pretzel, drizzled in dark and white chocolate, and we laughed as we each tore a piece off and fed them to each other. I heard Shelly snapping away in the background as Roger again stood on his chair, making another announcement.

"Surprise number five, the couple's first dance! I talked with the groom about what it should be, and when he told me, the rest was up to me! I enlisted the help of one of my friends, Adelaide, to sing it for you! Cecelia and Mattias, if you would, please take the center of the floor." Adelaide Andrews! Singing at our wedding! I wasn't quite as impressed as Shelly was. I could hear her squealing loudly beside me.

It was nightfall, and the terrace was lit up with yellow lighting from the ceiling. It had a romantic effect, as if candlelight was filling the room, bouncing off the tiles and onto our faces. Under the beautifully tiled ceiling, Mattias took me in his arms and pulled me close, as we had been so many times before. This time was extra special. I knew I could keep him for the rest of my life. Someone appeared in the corner of my eye, a beautiful woman in a lavishly decorated ballgown fit for a French court. She began singing "Nessun Dorma," and her voice was so rich and echoed so beautifully around us, that I started crying. Mattias kissed me again, and I told him not to ever stop. My parents, Brad and Shelly, and the Levanders soon surrounded us, four couples swaying to Puccini's masterpiece.

When Adelaide had finished, she got a roaring ovation from anyone who had been in earshot of her. By now, all the random park guests had wandered into our romantic atmosphere, and those who were in couples had started slow dancing along with us. So many people were there that I couldn't count them all. I could still smell hot dogs, and knew the vendors were having a blast.

Shelly walked up beside me and whispered, "Surprise number six!"

Roger stood back up on his chair, clearly loving the attention. "Attention ladies and gentlemen of New York! Me cousins, Shelly and Brad, have rented out a DJ for the remainder of the evenin'. Feel free to stay all night and party hard!"

The lights blacked out for a few seconds, and when they came back on, only half of them were lit. The rest of the lighting came from some neon lights that had been placed at several locations, including either side of the terrace and in the middle. A heavy beat dropped, and the crowd started jumping up and down wildly about, including Mattias and me. It reminded me a lot of our night at the rave, and I wondered if Mattias had something to do with this as well.

We danced for what felt like forever, with no sign of anyone looking tired. I looked over at my parents, who were dancing like crazy, their arms flailing about like wild teenagers. I laughed as I noticed Peter doing some sort of weird hop-in-place move. He was certainly not accustomed to unstructured dancing. The Levanders seemed to be doing some version of the Charleston. Shelly and Brad were still slow dancing, and on that note, I whispered to my husband, "How about we go back to our room now?"

As we snuck away indiscreetly into the night, we couldn't run across the park fast enough. Laughing and kissing and pulling the flowers out of my hair, my curls unwound and flowed around me. Mattias swept me up in his arms and twirled around, chiffon and flower petals fluttering around us. We raced back to the hotel to enjoy each other thoroughly and unabashedly.

Epilogue

I had not seen my seagull since the time in Abisko, and Mattias had not seen him since before our second time together in Sweden. I hoped he was all right, but I knew that he was. Birdie had served his purpose, a huge job for such a little bird. He'd watched over Charlie and me, comforted me in my time of grief, helped me adjust to a new life in a new place, and helped me to lead Mattias to God. To say he had been a reliable friend throughout my life was an understatement.

We didn't go on a honeymoon after our wedding. We decided we had visited enough places for quite a while. Instead, we chose to stay at home and enjoy married life. Right after we were married, my landlord mentioned in passing that he was retiring and moving to Florida to be with his grandkids. He said he wanted to give us the first opportunity to buy one or both properties since I had been such a dependable tenant.

I talked it over with Mattias, and we decided we should buy both and convert them into his-and-hers galleries. Hurriedly, we did this in a matter of weeks because three months after we got married we also got pregnant. We turned the guest bedroom back into a bedroom, a nursery this time. Overjoyed, Mattias chose a nautical theme so that our son would feel more at home in his

Scandinavian heritage. He painted glorious murals of the mountains and waterfalls of Norway on two of the walls.

My being pregnant inspired a whole new level of creativity in Mattias, and he began writing music again. This time the melodies were happier and more uplifting. He wanted our son to have something to listen to in the womb. Mattias could hardly contain his excitement of our life. Our days overflowed with laughter and happiness. And peanut butter. I uncontrollably craved peanut butter in all forms. Mattias became good at making thick, chunky peanut butter cookies with peanut butter cups in them, and I easily gained at least twenty pounds just from eating them.

In addition to his baking skills, his art also changed. He started a series of abstract pregnancy paintings, with me as his model. The paintings began to take on familiar images as the light glowed around my stomach. In my favorite one, there was a light behind my womb. The baby was in shadow but clearly reaching out in contrast to the brightness around him.

Mattias slept better now, as did I. Long gone were the nightmares of our past heartbreaks. As my belly grew outward, so did our love grow for each other. I would often wake up to Mattias' long, strong arms reached around me, his warm hands feeling for a sign of movement from inside.

We worked furiously, trying to get Mattias' gallery filled and properly advertised before I gave birth. His exhibition in New York had gone fantastically well, and he had received even more commissions from it. We chose to keep a few of the paintings out of his exhibition, the ones we felt were of the more personal moments that portrayed his spiritual journey and transformation. We proudly hung these in our apartment. "Never forget where you came from," I told him. "That's what keeps you humble."

Mama, Astrid, and Shelly had all taken turns flying in to help us get set up, and almost a year to the date of our wedding anniversary I gave birth to a healthy baby boy. He was big, and he would one day easily be as tall as his daddy. He had light brown hair and deep dark blue eyes just like Mattias. We named him Gregory Charles, after Mattias' first son and after Charlie.

We had gotten pregnant with our second child four months after Gregory Charles was born. Astrid was staying with us the day we found out the news. She had gone to the doctor's office with me while Mattias watched the galleries. I had to tell her first because I couldn't stop crying the entire way back to the apartment. I didn't know if it was postpartum, happiness, exhaustion, or a combination of the three that was causing me to be a babbling brook.

I kept a small picture of Charlie on my dresser, and it comforted me to talk to him occasionally. I told him about all the things I had done, how much he would've loved Norway. He heard all about Mattias, and how much he would've liked him.

I told Charlie I had looked up Mattias' name. It meant "God's gift," and it was the truest description after all that had happened. He would've loved to have been there to laugh at us screaming in the freezing water after I'd baptized Mattias.

"So that's this week. I'm having a lot of aches and pains, but the doctors say that's normal as my body adjusts to being pregnant again so soon. You'd really love baby Charlie, he laughs all the time and he's got adorable little dimples. We decided to call him Charlie, Gregory or Charles just doesn't seem like his personality. I know I've said it before but I think you'd really like Mattias too. He's amazing at everything. He runs both galleries when I can't. He bakes cookies and makes dinner. He runs hot baths for me and rubs my swollen feet.

"I didn't think I'd be happy again after you died. I miss you so much, but I still feel you sometimes. Certain things Mattias will say, or a glance Charlie will give me and they remind me of you somehow. I hope you're having a lot of fun in Heaven. Oh! And don't say anything, but I haven't told Mattias I'm pregnant yet. You're the second one to know!"

I was smiling at Charlie's picture as Mattias walked in. He was used to me talking to Charlie by now, so he just accepted it as one of my quirks and moved on. He came over and gave me the sweetest kiss.

"Hey Beauty, how'd the doctor's appointment go?"

I started crying as I told him we were pregnant again.

Though unplanned, Mattias and I were ecstatic about our second pregnancy because our children would be close in age and have each other to rely on. Or rather, Mattias was overjoyed, and I was exhausted. My body was still bloated and sore, and now we were going through the whole process again. I didn't mind, not really. Gregory was the most angelic baby I'd ever seen, and it thrilled me that they would have each other. I got overwhelmed and started crying again, my sixth time of the day. Mattias kissed my forehead and wrapped me tight in his strong arms. Right after telling him the news, my phone rang. It was an unknown number, from an area code I didn't recognize.

"Hello?"

"Hello, is this Cecelia Sweeting?"

"Yes, it is. May I ask who's calling?"

"I've been trying to find you for months! I kept hassling the hospital until finally they gave me a name and the location, and I found your parents in the phone book. I explained to your mother, and she gave me your number."

"The hospital? My parents? What's going on? Are they okay?"

"Yes, I'm sorry. Let me back up. My name is Sandra Parker. I'm from South Carolina. Several years ago, my son, Nathan, had surgery. He was born with a genetic disease, and it caused his kidneys to shut down." Why she was calling me about this was a mystery, but she continued.

"He had been receiving dialysis for years, but he was almost out of time unless he received a donor transfer. He was on the critical list. Cecelia, that's why I'm calling. He received your husband's kidneys."

I nearly dropped the phone, but I regained my composure. I put the phone on speaker and laid it down on the counter. "It's all confidential, all the records at the hospital, but I kept badgering them because I just had to tell you his story. He made a full recovery, and he's perfectly healthy now. I wanted to thank you from the bottom of my heart for your generous donation. Your husband was a perfect match for him, both in age and blood type, so it was as if my son never lost any time at all. He's just graduated from law school and gotten engaged, and it's all thanks to your husband. He's going to be an adoption attorney, bringing new families together." I was in tears as Mattias wrapped his arms around me.

"Cecelia, one more thing before I go. It may not be anything, but I feel like I should tell you anyway. Nathan changed some after his surgery. He wasn't an outdoors person before. He was studious and stayed indoors mostly, learning whatever he could. After he started to heal, he insisted on going outside and feeding the birds on our back porch. And he insisted that I go to all the thrift stores until I found him a denim jacket. He never wore one before his surgery. I know it's weird, but does that mean anything to you?"

By now I had lost it and was crying uncontrollably. Mattias picked up the phone now, saying, "Yes, it means a great deal more to her than you could know. Thank you so much for calling."

Made in the USA
Columbia, SC
20 July 2020

14009575R00159